ANOTHER LOVE

Erzsébet Galgóczi

Translated by
Ines Rieder and Felice Newman

CLEIS PRESS

Published in the United States by Cleis Press Inc., P.O. Box 8933, Pittsburgh, Pennsylvania 15221, and P.O. Box 14684, San Francisco, California 94114 by arrangement with Artisjus Agence Litteraire, Theatrale et de Musique du Bureau Hongrois pour la Protection des Droits d'Auteur, Budapest, Hungary.

Published in Hungarian as *Törvényen belül*, Szépirodalmi Könyvkiadó, Budapest, 1980.

Published in German as *Eine andere Liebe*, Neuer Malik Verlag, Kiel, 1986.

Printed in the United States.
Cover and text design: Cecilia Brunazzi
Cover photograph of the character Eva Szalánczky from the film *Another Way*, Hungaro Films; distributed by European Video Distributors.
Typesetting: CaliCo Graphics
Logo art: Juana Alicia

Library of Congress Cataloging-in-Publication Data

Galgóczi, Erzsébet, 1930—
    [Törvényen belül. English]
    Another love / by Erzsébet Galgóczi ; translated by Ines Rieder & Felice Newman.
        p.   cm.
    Translation of : Törvényen belül.
        ISBN: 0-939416-52-2 (cloth) : $24.95. — ISBN: 0-939416-51-4 (paper) : $8.95
    I. Title.
PH3241.G27T6813   1991
894' .51133—dc20   91-35664
                                     CIP

ACKNOWLEDGMENTS

S everal people helped us to bridge differences of language and culture. We wish to thank Laura Schiff, who translated selected portions from the original Hungarian edition; Z Budapest, who shared her experience with the Hungarian lesbian community and her memories of conversations with Erzsébet Galgóczi; Katalin Kátai told us about Galgóczi's publishing history.

Special thanks to Frédérique Delacoste, who remembered the film and pushed for the book, and to Alison Read, who found photographs from the film and gave Ines a careful, critical reading of the translation.

Many thanks to friends who read our manuscript in its many drafts: Frédérique Delacoste, Marlene Rodrigues, Lisa Frank, and Cleis' publishing intern, Keren Kurti.

INSIDE AND OUTSIDE THE LAW:
An Introduction to Erzsébet Galgóczi's Hungary

E rzsébet Galgóczi's *Another Love* was first published in
Hungary in 1980. Galgóczi chose to write about both
a lesbian love affair and the politically controversial events
of 1956, which she saw as a revolution. Nearly a decade
before the people of Eastern Europe began to challenge
and finally overthrow political parties which had held
power since World War II, Erzsébet Galgóczi confronted
her country's recent past in a bold and poignant novel.

Like Eva Szalánczky, *Another Love's* main character,
Erzsébet Galgóczi grew up in rural Western Hungary. Both
Eva Szalánczky and Erzsébet Galgóczi were born into peasant families in the early thirties. Both joined the Communist
Party (CP) in their youth, and both crossed class lines by
moving to Budapest and attending university. Both were
chain-smokers and heavy drinkers. And both fell in love
with straight women.

Neither Eva nor Erzsébet was unique in this regard. Very
few Hungarian women identified as "leszbikus." Even in
the seventies and eighties, when Budapest was dubbed
Eastern Europe's Castro District, most practicing lesbians
socialized with their friends in private and most preferred
to think of themselves as straight or bisexual.

When *Another Love* was made into a film in 1982, no
Hungarian actress wanted to take the part of Eva or Livia.
The Hungarian film industry has received subsidies from
a government that has spent great sums to promote mass
culture, and Hungarian filmmakers—including a number
of women directors—have gained international recognition. Despite this, and because of rumors of the many les-

1

bians and gay men in the Hungarian film industry, no one wanted to be associated with a lesbian character. No wonder then, that Jadwiga Jankowska-Cieślak and Grazyna Szapolowska from Poland were engaged to play Eva and Livia. That same year, Jadwiga Jankowska-Cieślak received the prize for best actress at the Cannes Film Festival.

When the film was first released in Hungary, it was an instant success. Karoly Makk, the filmmaker, said in an interview that he "was particularly interested in the mix of sexual and political deviation. The hero is a woman who is courageous enough to lead a different sexual life—but for only too obvious reasons she has to hide it."

This "different sexual life" paralleled the author's, since *Another Love* is a semi-autobiographical novel. But Erzsébet Galgóczi, one of Hungary's most outstanding *and* outspoken writers, opened a political can of worms with each book she published. Among Galgóczi's "political deviations" were her strong opinions on land reform and forced collectivization in Hungary, especially during the late forties and early fifties, the period when Eva Szalánczky (and Galgóczi) came of age. Several characters in *Another Love* talk about the effect of land reform on their lives.

Drawing heavily on her own experiences, and her own political analyses, Galgóczi invites us to take a look at this and other aspects of Hungarian history, culture and politics and to come to a better understanding of the post World War II period. Since Eva Szalánczky's search for a way to express her intellectual and sexual identities is the most important theme of *Another Love*, it is difficult to understand her without taking a closer look at some of the historical and political issues raised by the novel.

Erzsébet Galgóczi was born twelve years after the end of World War I, and a year after the 1929 stock market crash. Each of those events had a serious impact on the Hungarian

2

economy, even though they were felt more in the cities than in the rural areas where most Hungarians traditionally lived. None of the battles of World War I were fought on Hungarian soil and the country was not physically damaged. But the end of the war brought the end of the Austria-Hungarian monarchy. Hungary lost much of its territory and population to existing countries, like Romania, or new states created after the war, like Czechoslovakia and Yugoslavia.

The basic economic structure, though, was not touched. Hungary remained primarily an agricultural country. Although the short-lived Bèla Kun government attempted land reform in 1919, the situation of the peasants remained pretty much as it had been for generations.

Four thousand large estate holders controlled more than one-third of the land. Western Hungary, the region Erzsébet Galgóczi grew up in, was dominated by the Esterházy family, who owned more than 400 villages, 60 towns and 21 castles. In addition to the aristocratic land owners, there were 2 million land owners with small holdings, and nearly as many landless peasants. A large proportion of this rural proletariat was forced to live in conditions of extreme misery, often near starvation.

From 1920 until 1944, Hungary was ruled by Admiral Miklós Horthy, who was typical of the right-wing strong men who ruled many European states—from the Mediterranean to the Baltic. Horthy never pushed for reforms, and the land remained in the hands of a few big landowners.

Hungary began the thirties with a trade balance annihilated by the collapse of the world wheat market. Peasants, like Erzsébet Galgóczi's family, were left literally penniless. In the thirties, the country aligned itself with Italy and Germany. Hungary submitted to Germany's political domination at the same time it attempted to exploit the alliance as a way of regaining some of the territory lost after World

War I. Hungary tried to stay out of World War II as long as possible; nevertheless, it allowed German troops to cross its territory.

Ultimately, all the maneuvering was in vain. Hungary entered the war in 1941, and in October 1944, the Germans occupied the country and put the leader of the fascist Arrow Cross movement in charge. By then, Soviet troops were far inside the country, slowly driving back the Germans and their Hungarian allies. Hungary was devastated by this war in which over half a million Hungarians lost their lives. Budapest, the scene of house-to-house fighting between the Germans and the Soviets, was in ruins. The war left 9 out of 10 factories at least partially destroyed; 85 percent of all dwellings were seriously damaged or demolished. Practically all forms of transport were destroyed and communications were wrecked. The retreating Germans had destroyed all the bridges over the Danube, and had taken all the country's portable wealth. The Soviet army, on the other hand, lived off the land; later the Soviet Union took its share of repatriation in kind.

By the spring of 1945, the Red Army had defeated the last German soldiers on Hungarian territory. Once in control, the Soviets ordered a land reform. Most of the aristocratic feudal landowners lost their estates and many defected to the West. In 1948, an intensive phase of collectivization began which lasted until 1953. By March 1953, nearly 40 percent of the arable land was collectivized, and the previously private farmers had become members of producers' cooperatives.

Free elections were called in November 1945 to replace the provisional government. The Smallholders' Party gained an absolute majority over the Social Democrats and the Communists. But under pressure from the occupying Soviets, the Ministry of the Interior, controlling the police, was given to a Communist Party member, Imre Nagy, who held this post until 1946 when he was succeeded by László Rajk. New elections were held in 1947 and the CP gained the majority with 22 percent of the vote. The Smallholders' Party had split into several factions, none of them gaining enough votes on their own. Voters could use replacement ballots while traveling, and many CP members took that opportunity to go on a trip.

The new CP-controlled government pushed through all kinds of reforms, including land reform and nationalization of the entire school system, which until then had been mostly in the hands of the Catholic Church. The single most influential person at this time was the first secretary of the Hungarian CP, Mátyás Rákosi, the architect of a system, says First Lieutenant János Marosi, *Another Love's* protagonist and off-duty sleuth, that "instills fear" even after his regime has ended. Not only a hard-liner in his own right, Rákosi was closely allied with Stalin, an alliance which dated back to his many years in exile in Moscow. Imitating the Moscow show trials against imagined "enemies of socialism," Rákosi ordered fellow Party member László Rajk and some of his followers tried for allegedly conspiring with Yugoslavia's Tito and the West to re-establish capitalism in Hungary. Tito had been expelled from the Soviet bloc after advocating a different road to socialism.

There were probably many reasons for Rákosi's dislike for Rajk. Unlike Rákosi, Rajk was respected by the Party's rank and file. Rajk had not spent time in Moscow and was therefore connected to more independent and more liberal circles of communists in his own country as well as abroad.

The wave of Hungary's show trials lasted well into 1952. About 400,000 Hungarians were imprisoned during that period. Among those arrested and tried in 1951 was János Kádár who was to become the Party's secretary general in 1956, a position he held until 1988, one year before his death. By having Eva Szalánczky's editor-in-chief, Ferenc Erdös, arrested the same year as Kádár, Erzsébet Galgóczi lets the reader know that Erdös does not belong to the Party's Stalinist faction, but to those who, together with Kádár, held powerful positions in the post-1956 Hungary.

By 1952, Rákosi's power was complete: he presided over both the government and the Party. However, after Stalin's death in March 1953, Rákosi's power waned. Stalin's death left a big gap in the Party leadership not only in the Soviet Union, but also in those countries whose parties were closely aligned with it. This was the beginning of a period of political instability which lasted until 1956.

Various factions within the political parties of Eastern Europe and the Soviet Union began to vie for power. Since the Party determined these countries' governments, these shifts in power affected not only the organization of the parties, but the countries as a whole. Within the Soviet Communist Party, the conflict was temporarily ameliorated by putting a triumvirate in charge, one of them Nikita Khrushev. In July 1953, Imre Nagy, a protégé of Khrushev, became Hungary's new prime minister. He promised a new course: the end of the forced development of heavy industry, increased production of consumer goods, release of political prisoners and closing of internment camps. He also revised the collectivization plans and ordered a stop to the policy of forcing peasants to join producers' cooperatives.

People who had been in opposition to the parties' tight grip—among them many socialists and leftists—saw this as a unique opportunity to dismantle the structures built by Stalin and his clique. From East Germany and Czechoslovakia in 1953 to Poland and Hungary in 1956, people took to the streets. The protests were sparked by rising food prices, the lack of democracy within the unions, and the unchecked power of the Party.

In Hungary, the Party's rank-and-file membership was no longer willing to accept Stalinist leadership. In 1953, Imre Nagy, considered a liberal communist, became Hungary's prime minister, and others of his faction attained positions of power—but control of the armed forces remained in the hands of the Stalinists.

Throughout what was then politically defined as Eastern Europe, the years after Stalin's death were marked with debates about the future course of the Soviet Union and its allies. The average citizen in the West knew little or nothing about those discussions. Only Khrushev's revelations at the XX Party Congress in February 1956 reached an international audience. While seen by many as the beginning of a de-Stalinization process, insiders claim that Khrushev's speech actually indicated the *end* of a more liberal era.

In the fall of 1955, the Hungarian Party's Stalinist faction made one last attempt to regain its lost power. Imre Nagy was dismissed as prime minister in the spring of 1955 and shortly afterwards expelled from the Party. Mátyás Rákosi was reinstated. Prominent communist writers, scientists and artists objected to the return of the rule of force and organized against Rákosi. This was the beginning of open disagreement with the Party leadership.

During those years, Erzsébet Galgóczi finished her studies and lived in the capital. Given her privileged position and her involvement in politics, she, too, took sides. Only a future biography might bring to light the full extent of her ideas, reflections and actions in the fifties. We have only her novels, published in the eighties, as a guide. In them, she reveals her deeply-felt resentment of the Party's policies in regard to the peasants and the intellectuals.

In *Another Love*, the year 1956 is regarded as a line of demarcation: characters, typical of Hungarians, speak of "before 1956" and "after 1956." Early that year, the Petöfi

7

Circle, named for a heroic, nationalist poet who died in the Hungarian revolution of 1848, was founded. Included were the intellectuals who had protested Rákosi's return to power the previous year, along with students and members of the Party's youth organization. These intellectuals did not advocate feudalism or capitalism, but favored a multiparty system such as the one Hungary had enjoyed from 1945 to 1947. To this government, they felt they owed the agrarian reform and the nationalization of key industries, banks and schools.

In March 1956, political pressure forced Rákosi to rehabilitate the victims of the Rajk trials and all the surviving prisoners were released. That same political pressure caused the government to order the removal of all the mine fields and barbed wire along Hungary's western borders in May 1956.

In the first half of June, the Petöfi Circle held a number of public meetings, each attended by several thousand people. They understood their organizing as an open declaration of war on the current Party leadership. In July 1956, the Party's Central Committee dismissed Rákosi, this time from all his offices and in disgrace.

That same month, László Rajk was reburied in Budapest's Central Cemetery. More than 250,000 people attended the funeral, thus turning it into a powerful demonstration.

At the beginning of October, Nagy asked to be readmitted to the Party and the politburo granted his request. On October 23, 1956, students in Budapest staged a peaceful demonstration in general support of the demands raised by intellectuals and Party reformers. Ernö Gerö, a Stalinist who replaced Rákosi as Party general secretary, spoke to the crowd. When his speech was not well-received, he ordered the police to fire into the crowd. Within twenty-four hours, the demonstration had turned into a popular, armed uprising. There were two main demands: retreat of the

Soviet Army, which had occupied Hungary since the war, and free elections.

Heavy fighting lasted for days. The Hungarian Army joined the people and handed out weapons. The Soviet troops were driven out of the capital. A general strike was called and for weeks the country was paralyzed.

In accordance with popular demand, the Party asked Imre Nagy and his faction to form a coalition government until elections could be held. The Soviet troops had withdrawn to the Hungarian-Soviet border, and Nagy announced that he was negotiating for their complete evacuation of the country. On November 1, Hungary withdrew from the Warsaw Pact and declared itself a neutral state. This was too much of a risk for the delicate cold war balance, and Soviet troops returned to Budapest. They entered the city on November 4th. Imre Nagy and his government took refuge in the Yugoslavian embassy. Later, he was tried and, in June 1958, he was executed. János Kádár, who had been imprisoned under Rákosi, formed a so-called revolutionary peasant-worker government.

In the aftermath of these events, almost 200,000 people fled to the West. Since the mines along the border to the West had been removed earlier, and since the Hungarian Army was no longer patrolling the border regions, it was possible for many people to walk or drive into Austria. The Soviet Army had little detailed knowledge of the region and wasn't able to keep people from leaving, especially at night.

The following years witnessed many fierce debates about the political meaning of the November 1956 events in Hungary. There are those—most often the hard-liners—who referred and still might refer to that period as a counter-revolution, because any revolt against a state that claims to be based on Marxism/Leninism is a counter-revolution. There are those who don't want to commit themselves and call the events an uprising. And then there are those, like Gal-góczi, who defined the events of 1956 as a revolution or revolutionary period.

Perhaps Hungary was the first powerful reminder that Europe's borders were defended by cold war lords and that it would take more than popular force to change them. Among the cold war lords are the U.S. and its allies. The stubborn U.S. cold war mentality may have prevented the possibility of liberal changes and may have solidified the so-called iron curtain, which might have been a short-lived reality. But the strategists of the cold war did not want to risk any geopolitical changes in the heart of post-World War II Europe.

At first, the Party did not retaliate. But after a few months, people were arrested and tried for their participation in the revolt of 1956. Eva's loneliness after losing her entire social network to the events of 1956 indicates the extent of the arrests. The Party, officially called the Hungarian Workers Party, was dissolved, and all its 900,000 members were expected to reapply for membership in the newly-found Hungarian Socialist Workers Party. Half a year later, less than 300,000 had asked for readmittance. Many, like Eva Szalánczky, chose to wait and see what new political developments the future would bring. The Party never managed to regain its pre-1956 numbers, despite all the privileges of membership.

The Writers' and Journalists' Unions were suspended in January 1957, and all the prominent "revisionist" writers and journalists were arrested for counter-revolutionary plotting. Forced collectivization, which had slowed down, was sped up in 1958, and by 1961, 90 percent of all arable land was collectively owned, compared to less than 40 percent in September 1956.

The terror of the secret police, which peaked during the Rajk trials, did not return in the years following 1956, but the government admitted the continued existence of concentration camps. On January 1, 1958 a decree was issued stating that anyone who wanted to obtain or keep any of the more important jobs needed a "certificate of good behavior."

Eva Szalánczky was shot while trying to cross the border at the beginning of September 1959. At the end of that month, the ban on the Hungarian Writers' Union was lifted, but one still understood that "all literary activities must support the state in building socialism." By the time *Another Love* was published, the Party had consolidated power to such a degree that it no longer considered a "different" view of the past a danger. It was nearly a decade, from 1980 to late 1989, before the parties in the Soviet-allied countries lost their power. Since Erzsébet Galgóczi died in May 1989, she never saw the collapse of a system that had made the lives of people like Eva Szalánczky so miserable and, ultimately, not worth living.

Ines Rieder
Vienna, Austria
September 1991

THE PASSIONATE LANDSCAPE OF EVA SZALANCZKY:
An Introduction to *Another Love*

"**I** don't care if you are an informer," says Eva Szalánczky, "What could you say about me?" Eva Szalánczky is an idealist's idealist. Her greatest sorrow is that since her stories are not read in the morning newspaper, she is not in danger of being interrogated for their content.

"That would at least prove I have thoughts . . ." Eva is an investigative reporter whose editor feeds her assignments, even though he knows her stories are too hot to publish.

Eva is too honest, too indignant, too passionate to keep her mouth shut. Plus she's having an affair with the boss' mistress.

Eva Szalánczky is revealed to us through letters, scribbled bits of journal entries, and the memories of the people whose lives she has touched. No one recalls her dispassionately. No one forgets Eva Szalánczky, especially not her fictional counterbalance, First Lieutenant János Marosi, the unheroic sleuth who investigates her death.

Eva's the only woman Marosi's ever loved (or so he thinks) and the only woman he'll never have.

If this sounds like detective fiction camp, well, at moments it reads that way. But *Another Love* is more than a lesbian rendition of scenarios made popular by Raymond Chandler, Dashiell Hammett or James Cain, authors familiar to Erzsébet Galgóczi's readers.

Why did Galgóczi choose the detective novel as her vehicle for exploring the political and sexual themes of *Another Love*? For starters, Galgóczi is recreating the fifties, which in Eastern Europe were hard-boiled years. These were politically dangerous times for intellectuals. "Between Christmas 1952 and March 1958, I hardly wrote any stories—and what I wrote wasn't good, and what might have been good, wasn't published," she later wrote.

The landscape of the detective novel provides a setting for years entrenched in secrecy, suspicion, and double meanings. One could hardly accuse *Another Love* of looking at the past from a cozy distance. Though Galgóczi assumed (and did not hide) her lesbianism, she surely experienced the secrecy, suspicion, and double meanings imposed upon gay life as well.

Galgóczi's choice of the genre of detective fiction may have been a matter of political expediency. While Galgóczi was as idealistic a critic of her times as Eva Szalánczky, Galgóczi attained a success that would have made Szalánczky suspicious. Erzsébet Galgóczi was a survivor, a writer who received national recognition, several prestigious prizes, and was elected general secretary of the Hungarian Writers Union. Perhaps the format of a mystery provided Galgóczi with the perfect cover. She could explore the riddle of 1956 (revolutionary uprising or counter-revolutionary conspiracy?) by cloaking her story in mystery.

Another Love is not Galgóczi's only detective story; among her many publications are several political mysteries crafted from real life murders and suicides. ". . . Reality offers the best stories," Galgóczi writes in an autobiographical essay, "I have only to observe all these conflicts and fill them out with flesh and blood." In this essay, found in an anthology on the experience of Hungarian writers since World War II, Galgóczi writes openly of her inability to create and publish in the fifties. She describes the misery her family suffered under strict agricultural policies. She tells of losing her university scholarship after fighting a decision which denied her classmates and herself a promised year of study in the Soviet Union.

Finally, Galgóczi—no loyal Party hack, but a strong believer in communist ideals—chose genre fiction simply because she wanted to reach the largest possible audience. No longer a starving student, the post-fifties Galgóczi was a published mystery writer.

Another Love stands among Galgóczi's most popular books; it sold about 50,000 copies, which was not unusual in Hungary prior to the fall of the Iron Curtain. Books were cheap in Hungary then. People read a lot—TV and radio took a back seat to books since the programs were lousy and you didn't trust the information anyway. Now, with the opening of the borders, there is more competition for people's attention spans. TV and radio news broadcasts are livelier, a greater variety of newspapers and magazines is available, and previously banned movies are now being shown.

If you could get a book published, however, it would generally appear uncensored (since censorship occurred at the level of editorial selection) and 20,000 to 50,000 copies would be passed from hand to hand, a guaranteed substantial audience. Compare this to the United States, where it is not uncommon for a novel to be published with a 5,000-copy first printing, half of which may be remaindered after six months. The question was who got published and who *decided* who got published. Galgóczi—writer, lesbian, outspoken critic—managed this system well.

So. What was Galgóczi trying to tell us?

I read *Another Love* as a parable of Hungary in 1959. For me, the characters in this detective novel represent features of a political and emotional landscape.

Hungary is a land of many deprivations, like Eva, deserving of "work that would bring joy . . . success, comfort, travel, a home and love." Invaded by its "benefactor" state, like a child eaten by its parent, Hungary itself is aptly described by an old Budapest saying: "I'm hungry. I'm thirsty. I'm tired. I'm cold and I need to *piss.*"

The casualty in this struggle for survival is honesty. While Eva upholds the virtue to an absurd degree, the others in her story seem to stumble from one rationalization to another.

Even when she is arrested for making out with her lover in a public park ("I adore your mouth. It is a soft, single pleading: 'Come to me.'"), Eva straightens out the cop's version of reality: "We watched you for two hours. I've never seen such passion, and I'm from the vice squad. Must be a great love?" Never mind that he has just arrested the "great lovers", it's his curiousity and envy that matter.

"My dear man," begins a response that could be immortalized in the movies, "for someone working with the vice squad, you are pretty naïve . . ." What constitutes "great love," Eva instructs the poor fellow, does not take place on a park bench in winter.

"Compromises are like runs in a stocking," Eva warns. "They keep on running, and in the end the person is just one big run."

Here is a country telling lies to itself, a moral landscape littered with the spiritual equivalents of cigarette butts and cognac bottles. Where a police psychologist, explaining the inevitable tragedy of Eva's "case" (read: lesbianism), raves against the hypocrisy of Hungarian intellectuals. "There have never been so many divorces, suicides, never so much alcoholism and so little work and success," he says after offering Marosi an illicit mid-day vodka ("It's not allowed during working hours, but I was the one who offered . . .").

"You know," confesses one of Eva's co-workers, "my generation went through so much, it is almost a miracle that we are not more rotten than we actually are. I gave up believing in anything a long time ago, least of all the written word . . ."

16

And what's happened to the press? The newspapers print babble, according to Eva, because Party ideology supersedes empirical reality. But you can't trust empirical reality either (read: "objective" reporting) because everybody lies to the press. This is a place where a newspaper reporter can't even get a county agricultural agent to answer a few questions honestly.

"But I don't lie," says Eva, "and I can't stand other people's lies." Eva's unwillingness to lie is costly. She can hardly expect to have a flourishing career—since her propensity to blurt out the truth means she cannot keep a job. Unemployment is a criminal offense in Hungary in 1959.

Unlike ID cards carried by Western Europeans, Eva's ID card lists the details of her employment (*None*). In Hungary in 1959, one must have a residence *and* an employer; otherwise one is liable to be arrested for vagrancy. But there is a catch: only Party members get good jobs. One day, the Party is disbanded; the next morning, there is a "new" Party. To join or not to join? What is the right choice?

In Galgóczi's view, Hungary is a nation caught in an Orwellian squeeze.

And Eva *is* Hungary's national spirit.

Another Love is Erzsébet Galgóczi's State of the Union address, and she has chosen a fiercely independent (albeit, emotionally battered) lesbian to carry the message.

"This country is *my* country, whether you like it or not," Eva declares.

Such guts, Galgóczi! In how many novels written in the "free" and "liberated" West does a lesbian character repre-represent the soul of a nation?

Here, a broken lesbian love affair is a metaphor for universal longings. The expression of dignity, of personal choice, of passionate freedoms—all are unattainable in Eva's world.

It's the end of summer. Ines Rieder and I FAX daily from the United States to Austria, back and forth, letters and notes on drafts of the translation . . . The actual manuscript has made the trip several times, across the Atlantic and back in the suitcases of tourists. The Soviet Union has deconstructed. Ines tells me what Eastern Europeans are saying, and the international gossip makes our press look like comic books. She writes of the "events" of 1989, 1990, 1991; like *1956*, these years will be spoken in italics, with a special inflection, an awareness of the possibilities (and limitations) of self-creation.

Like Eva—and Galgóczi—the world still hopes for change: "If a human being wants to become truly herself, if she wants to be a real person, with an individual and indispensable face, then she must not turn away from herself. She has to take her life into her own hands, the same way a sculptor takes material in hand, giving shape to an idea that emerged formlessly from his soul. This requires an incredible amount of courage. It's a path leading through crisis, doubt and uncertainties."

Felice Newman
Cleis Press/Pittsburgh
September 1991

1

On a storm-tossed night in September 1959, a military patrol fired on someone they observed trying to cross the border illegally in the district of Mohács. First Lieutenant Marosi was informed about the incident the following morning, upon returning from a sleepless night with his lover. The sergeant had already prepared a report. The corpse had been returned from the forest, had been laid out on the long table in the soldiers' barracks and covered with a clean sheet. Marosi disdained illegal border crossings—in the years before 1956, he had been witness to too many tragedies. His bad mood quickly turned to anger when he discovered that the victim was a young woman.

"The two young guys say there was a terrible storm—lots of thunder, crashing trees and pounding rain," tried the chubby-faced sergeant in defense of his people. "They barely saw the tips of their own noses; they only saw a scurrying shadow caught in the flashes of lightning. They yelled three times. Twice they fired in the air, but the woman did not halt. The two . . . in their fear—"

Marosi was dismayed: "If the thunder was really so loud, she couldn't have heard them yell, she couldn't even have heard the gunshots . . . Who are the two cowards?"

The sergeant gave him their names.

"These two had better not expect promotions for this!

When I'm done with them, they'll be sorry they were born boys!" cursed Marosi. "Isn't it possible to just arrest a young woman?"

"This handbag was found close to her." The sergeant pointed to a soaked bag, which, despite a layer of dirt, was recognizably dark blue. "She didn't have any luggage. Here is her identification card."

Marosi looked at the card. For a moment, he stopped breathing.

"Eva Szalánczky," he murmured. His face whitened. "I know an Eva Szalánczky . . ." He stared at the picture. It was a distorted picture, poorly printed, but he could recognize her.

"Terrible," he mumbled with a trembling voice, as he took the bag and staggered into his office.

He picked up a bottle of vodka and opened the dead woman's bag. He started with her papers.

Name: Eva Szalánczky

Born: 1931

Educational Level: University

Marital status: Single

Occupation: Journalist

Residence: Budapest, Verpeléti Street 38 (Boarder)

Employer: Currently none (Until June 1959, on the editorial staff of *People and Culture*)

Marosi looked at the photo one more time. It showed a faintly smiling woman with short hair, her head slightly tilted. She squinted distrustfully at the camera, with world-weary eyes that contradicted her timid smile. In the picture, she wore a white blouse with an open collar. *Oh my god, how much she liked those shiny white blouses with their broad collars—Petőfi used to wear such collars . . .* Marosi opened the dirty blue handbag and took out a crushed packet of cigarettes and a matchbox with broken edges. It was as if he could see the young woman in front of him. She never gestured while talking, but her hands always played with something, a matchbox, a fountain pen, a toothpick, the fringes of a tablecloth, a cognac glass . . .

The bag further contained a Parker pen, cuticle scissors, a comb, tweezers, a mirror, a pocketknife, a small bar of soap wrapped in a used envelope, a small lavender bottle, two handkerchiefs, two headache pills and a current appointment book containing some notes and an alphabetized section for addresses. Marosi put the appointment book in the inner pocket of his jacket, disregarding service regulations.

In addition, the bag held a few folded sheets of stationery of excellent quality, a leather purse with nine hundred and seventy forints, a permanent museum pass, and a train ticket from Budapest to Mohács with the previous day's stamp. First Lieutenant Marosi put everything back into the bag. Intuition told him to unfold the seemingly unused stationery. The following was written on the center sheet: "Mohács, September 8th, 1959. There is no explanation. One cuts open one's veins . . . Someone else comes along who will explain it."

In order to discover this explanation, First Lieutenant Marosi asked for a leave of absence. He had to wait ten days, since there was no available substitute for him.

2

Marosi called from the Southern Railway Station in Budapest.

"Still not married?" he asked when the phone was answered by a pleasant, somewhat sleepy woman's voice.

"Who's calling?"

"Don't you recognize my voice, Cunika? I'm coming from Böhönye and I'm—"

"Jancsi! I can't believe!" Brief silence, followed by joyful excitement. "Where are you right now?"

"Still at the railway station."

"I'm acting tonight. But now I have time. Can you come by?"

She hasn't had a man for quite a while, thought Marosi, and he said: "Wait, Cunika. I have to take care of some business in Budapest, but nothing official. I need a place to stay. That's why I asked if you had gotten married."

"We'll figure it out," said the woman, after reflecting for a moment, and then added in an angry tone: "You've always been a dirty materialist."

It was eleven o'clock in the morning and the fall sun was out. The leaves of the mighty chestnut trees on Erzsébet Szilágy Alley had turned to their fall colors; their fruits, thorny on the outside, but silken inside, had burst and had begun spurting out their ripe flesh. Sitting in the cab, Marosi thought of the coming hours with excitement. He paid the driver, and carrying his suitcase, quickly ran up the three flights in the elegant apartment building. A fresh

22

young woman dressed in a silk robe patterned with big roses, with dyed blond hair and a rather curvy chest—her face a bit vulgar—opened the door. Marosi dropped his suitcase and embraced her in the hall. His hands moved over her big breasts and he could feel that she wore nothing underneath her robe. She hadn't even put on any lipstick, since she knew that he didn't like its taste, not even the taste of real expensive lipstick. "I want to kiss you, not the Elida company." Haltingly they kissed, like gourmets, who only nibble appetizers in order to increase their desire. But then silk and other fine fabrics became as intolerable as the hair shirts of penitents. The robe slid to the floor first, followed by jacket, tie and shirt. Marosi squeezed the insatiable body and carried her into the room to the unmade sofa bed. On the bed he took off his shoes and pants.

Being experienced lovers, they both enjoyed making love a great deal. They knew each other's bodies, appreciated each detail, and since each wanted absolute pleasure, they demanded no less from the other. Afterwards, they collapsed, exhausted like two empty wells.

"You are the only man in my life," the woman whispered with closed eyes, "who can hold it for such a long time . . . Too bad you don't love me."

Caught, Marosi put his hand on her chest, and felt her rapid heartbeat. *Every woman I've ever desired*, he thought, *I've had. Except for Eva Szalánczky.* Maybe because she was the only one he ever loved. But whenever he was with her, he felt ineffective, awkward, unpolished, resigned, never daring to think, *I have a right to you*, the way he felt with other women . . . *How stupid she had been! If only she had come to see me!* The ministry, his mother, everybody knew where he was stationed, everybody had his address. If it had been her irrevocable wish to leave, he would have taken her across the border without even expecting a nod of thanks. Now there was nothing he could do.

After a bath, he and Cunika sat in the dining room in their bathrobes, eating bacon and eggs. Cunika did not really keep house, she ate wherever and whenever she was hungry: mushrooms filled with goose liver at the Café Hungaria, or boiled beef with mustard at the corner butcher.

"What secret mission are you on? Can you talk about it?" she asked.

"It's no secret. I'm even asking *you* for help," said Marosi. "Do you remember Eva Szalánczky?"

"Why the hell shouldn't I remember her? We attended the same gymnasium in Püspökvár. And on top of it, she was a secretary of the Hungarian Youth Association. She even was the secretary of the Association's city committee. Everyone knew her—"

"That I know," Marosi interrupted, and added bitterly: "I knew her by then. But I want to know, when did you see her last?"

"In Budapest we didn't see each other. Only by accident." She took the dirty dishes to the sink, and returned with an open bottle of wine and a siphon bottle, and mixed two spritzers. All of a sudden, she looked at Marosi: "Why are you interested in this woman?"

Playing with some crumbs left on the table, Marosi told her the story. She listened with frightened, wide open eyes.

"That's terrible! Hideous!" she repeated. "Why would she do that? If she wanted to defect, why didn't she leave in 1956, like everyone else?"

"That's what I'd like to find out—and that's why I'm in Budapest."

Cunika took a sip of her spritzer and then looked sharply at the man: "And why do you want to know this? Were you in love with her?"

"Look," Marosi said, his head bent, "the three of us went on to university after attending a miserable provincial gymnasium. All three of us come from the working class. Your father was a factory worker . . ."

"Foreman," Cunika corrected him.

". . . Eva's father was a peasant, and mine was the village mason. All three of us managed to graduate. You became an actress; I, an army engineer; and Eva, after passing her teaching credentials, became a journalist. We live the lives of intellectuals. Given the same objective conditions, how come you made a career, I'm vegetating, and Eva's life hit the skids?"

"Career?!" The actress declined. "Only as long as my husband, that pimp, forced me into prostitution. Do you know how many film offers I've had since he defected? Not a single one!" Almost triumphantly, she went on: "I'm punished, because he abandoned his country. Even though everybody knows that we had been on bad terms during his last months here. He didn't even live here anymore."

Discouraged, Marosi kept silent. How good it would be if Cunika wouldn't immediately think of herself all the time. If only one could have a reasonable talk with her. On stage it was different; there, she could rely on someone else's words, but even then she would have to feel the inner logic of the dialogue in order to convince an audience. Maybe it was different . . . He allowed her to spill her superficial emotions on him, to blame her husband—the pimp—for making her sacrifice her youth to the film industry, only to leave her disgracefully after her youth had faded. Marosi went behind Cunika, put his arms around her, and dug his mouth in her neck.

"You are not bad off, Cunika. At least you got to keep this beautiful apartment . . . Eva Szalánczky, who never married, had to live as a boarder until she died."

Sulking, Cunika pulled the man's head toward her: "I know, I bore you already . . ."

"It's difficult to deny that," Marosi smiled. Then, in an entirely different tone of voice: "Can I make phone calls from here?"

25

"Sure." She also got up, stretched a bit, and did a few deep breathing exercises, alternating with waist twists and torso bends. She went to her bedroom. "Take the phone with you. I have to sleep for another hour . . . Did you bring your uniform?" she asked abruptly.

"Yes, I brought it with me," Marosi said, and remembered that he still had to unpack his suitcase. "Why do you ask?"

"You'll go to the theater with me tonight, won't you?"

Marosi knew that women liked to show off in his company. He was tall, athletic, with brown skin, classic Roman features and golden brown eyes under long black lashes— "brushwood fire burns in your eyes," Eva Szalánczky had once said to him—and shiny black hair. Women led him around like a thoroughbred.

"I don't want any mix-ups, dearest," he said in a pleasant voice. "I don't want any scandals with your current suitor to drive you to hysterics, and I don't want to be forced to kick in anyone's teeth. I don't have time for that."

Caught, Cunika showed him her glowing red tongue and closed the door to her room.

3

Notice of Eva Szalánczky's death had not been published in the papers; nevertheless, a small circle probably knew about it. Despite this, Marosi decided to proceed as if he had news from her. From where? Maybe from abroad?

The small list of addresses looked older than the appointment book to which it had been attached. It was obviously well used, its pages dog-eared and marked by fingerprints. Phone numbers were recorded in different pencils; some had been crossed out, others changed, and one page showed tracks of raindrops or tears.

Still, this address book couldn't be that old. With bitterness, Marosi thought that once his phone number had been in one of Eva's notebooks, way back when he attended university.

Besides the phone numbers of physicians, stores, libraries, and other necessities, Marosi found an additional eighteen names. Five listed only addresses, without phone numbers, among them the flat where Eva used to sublet a room. Was this a big or small circle of friends? Were these people friends or merely acquaintances? He would soon find out.

Marosi came across a bottle of cognac in Cunika's well-stocked bar. He placed it on the table, arranged the appointment book and his pen right next to it, made himself comfortable, and dialed the first number: Florian Arva.

"Yes," said an indifferent sounding woman's voice.

"Good afternoon. I would like to talk to Florian Arva."

There was a long silence. Far too long. Marosi thought the woman had left in order to fetch him. Then the same woman was back on the line, but her tone had changed:

"Who wants to talk to him?"

"First Lieutenant János Marosi."

"From the police? . . . What do you still want?" The voice wasn't angry, but rather apathetic.

Marosi was embarrassed, but only for a second.

"No, I'm not from the police. I'm an old military comrade of Flori."

"Marosi? . . . That's possible . . ." After a short pause: "Have you been dismissed?"

"Yes . . . that is . . ." Marosi stammered.

"Don't you know that they hanged my husband?"

"Hang—" Marosi lost his voice. Without missing a beat, the woman screamed into the phone:

"You damned informer! Don't you trip me up. It was in the newspapers. Everybody could read it! Even abroad! I'm not telling any state secrets! What do you still want from me? Why don't you leave me in peace? Haven't I been through enough? Do you have to break what's left of a human soul?" Her words were lost in muffled sobs.

Shocked, Marosi hung up. His whole body shivered as he stared at the phone. He had not expected such an introduction. That the first acquaintance of Eva Szalánczky—at least according to alphabetical order—had been hanged. When? Why? And who was this Florian Arva anyway? What was his connection to Eva? He had to find out the address. He had to go there and question the concierge. It was good that he had brought his uniform.

He poured himself a cognac, pulled himself together and dialed the next number. Magdolna Kóródi. Again, a woman picked up the phone. By the sound of her voice, she was middle-aged or possibly older.

"Good afternoon. I would like to talk to Magdolna."

"Magdolna . . ." the voice sounded hesitant. "Who wants to talk to her?"

"First Lieutenant Marosi." Disconcerted silence.

"Police?"

"No! I'm a military engineer. An old acquaintance of Magdolna."

"Oh, welcome, my engineer." The voice sounded amiable, as if on the lookout for a son-in-law. "I'm Magdolna's mother. You haven't seen her in a long time?"

"Unfortunately, it has been a long time. You know, my job keeps me in the provinces."

"My dear engineer, all I can give you is my daughter's address. In these troubled times . . ." Marosi could hear the woman's mood sour, ". . . she chose the 'free world.'"

Marosi stopped short.

"You mean she left illegally? . . . For what reason?"

"Do you think, my dear engineer, I know why? She is our only child. We gave her everything we could. Of course, it wasn't as much as her classmates got because I'm only a concierge and my husband is a driver. Nevertheless, she left twelve dresses in her closet. Is it worth it to start from scratch abroad? She had a good job in the gymnasium. But abroad—she is not complaining—she has only managed to find a job as a clerk in a gun store . . . I would like to believe that she has a better life there as a saleswoman than a university professor here. But is this the only thing that counts? Doesn't she care about her position in society?"

"Was she guilty of something in 1956? Is that the reason she left?"

"God forbid! She didn't do anything. We are not that kind of family," the woman said proudly. "Once she had to deal with the police, but they only wanted her as a witness. It had something to do with an acquaintance."

"You wouldn't remember the name of this acquaintance?"

"She mentioned the name then . . . but it doesn't come to mind now. It was nobody we saw regularly."

Marosi took a chance: "She didn't happen to know Eva Szalánczky?"

"Oh, yes. Eva was my daughter's classmate." There was a certain warmth in the woman's voice. "Eva often came over to study with my daughter, because she couldn't heat her student digs. She was a very poor girl, even during the winter she just wore a gabardine coat. I always asked her in vain to stay for supper."

"When did you see Eva last?"

"It has been a long time. The two were still at the university. Once she showed up late at night. Her eyes were all red from crying. My daughter wasn't at home and I invited her to sit down in the kitchen, because I was ironing. I asked her: 'What's the matter, Eva?' But she didn't give me an answer, only started crying again. Her handkerchief was all wet, and I gave her one of my freshly ironed ones . . . Then she left . . . After that, I never saw her again. It must have been half a year later when I asked my daughter about Eva. Then I wondered if they had had a fight, or if something had happened to her. My daughter told me that Eva had been sent to the province to work. By that point, they both had received their diplomas."

Interesting, Marosi thought. *Magdolna lied to her mother.* She must have known that Eva started working at the newspaper right after finishing her studies. That was in 1955. It's possible that she worked in the province later, but not at the time which Magdolna mentioned to her mother.

"Would you give me your daughter's address please?"

"Wait a second, I'll look for her last letter."

Marosi took down the Chicago address, thanked her and politely said good-bye to the concierge.

Did Eva return the handkerchief? Or does even a simple handkerchief bring joy to such a poor existence? Marosi wondered without particular reason and filled his glass with cognac. The silence was interrupted by shuffling noises and the sound of Cunika's humming. It was five-thirty, and he did not want to dial another number—he'd rather Cunika didn't overhear his conversations.

Cunika emerged from the bedroom in a flashy dress. With practiced dignity, she recited: "You are armed with friendly fire. *Peu à peu*, you have your way with me. You start with regular visits, and then you make all sorts of promises, followed by serenades, ballets, gifts. I resist them all, but you don't give up. Slowly, but surely, you get your way. I'm out of control. It's useless to try to fight it—marriage is inevitable . . . Please be so kind and call a cab."

"Marriage!" Marosi protested, while calling the cab. "But Cunika, with you in the capital, and me in Böhönye?"

"Could you manage to be sent to Budapest?" She waved—"Don't worry, no danger from my end."

"Then what was all that about?"

"That bullshit is tonight's performance!" she flared up. "The great actresses, the ones who have made it, the ones who get all the leading parts—from Julia to Jeanne d'Arc to Gertrude—claim that there are no supporting parts, only minor actresses. What a terrible piece of fiction. How can I beat Elisabeth Kása if she always gets the leading parts, and I'm only the maid?"

Marosi didn't understand anything about art, but he knew Elisabeth Kása. She was neither beautiful, nor ugly, nor interesting enough to be a star. She was like her face, a little bit ordinary, a bit insignificant.

"Could you leave me a key, dear?"

Cunika picked up a muslin shawl, put on her gray gabardine coat and kissed him good-bye. Marosi locked the door after her, made some coffee, drank some cognac, lit a cigarette, and then he dialed the next number: Livia Kismányoki.

A youthful woman's voice answered. In the background, he could hear a radio playing Hungarian folk music.

"Livia?" he asked.

"No. Who is calling?"

"My name is János Marosi. Good evening. Could I talk to Livia?"

"What is it about?"

"Oh, just something personal . . . I work in the province, but occasionally when in Budapest I see her."

"My sister can't come to the telephone. I'm sorry. She's in the hospital."

"Oh, I'm sorry! What's wrong?"

"Are you a journalist?" The voice sounded distrustful.

"Of course," said Marosi.

"For what paper?"

"*The Mohács People's Daily,*" Marosi lied easily.

"Your paper down there didn't get any news about it?"

"We heard a rumor . . . But I didn't want to believe it . . ."

"Still, it is true. Her husband shot her. With his service revolver." Marosi could feel his adrenalin flowing. Livia's sister seemed to feel important, having a place on the periphery of such an extraordinary event. "He wanted to kill her. Fortunately the bullet only hit her spine. They managed to operate on her."

"Terrible," Marosi said truthfully. "When did it happen?"

"A month ago. Yes, last Sunday was four weeks."

"When can I see her?"

"Any time." Readily, she gave him the hospital's address, the floor, the room number. "Livia will be pleased. You know how monotonous life in a hospital can be."

Marosi thanked her. He was happy to have found a clue. Most probably Eva Szalánczky and Livia Kismányoki had worked in the same office.

He had no further luck. He called the number next to a man's name, and he got an iron factory. Nobody knew Eva

Szalánczky there. He let the next number ring for a long time, but nobody answered. At the third number, he was told that Eva Szalánczky used to rent a room, but had moved out a long time ago. The person at the last number had defected.

The number next to the name Magda Módra belonged to a branch of the city's Ervin Szabó Library. There he was told that Comrade Módra—*Comrade* pronounced as if it had been underlined twice—had already gone home. She had no private phone.

It was seven o'clock. First Lieutenant Marosi put on the jacket of his uniform and locked the door of the unfamiliar apartment behind him.

4

A rather plump woman opened the door to her apartment on the third floor of a building on Verpeléti Street. She was in her early fifties, dressed in a yellow robe, with curlers in her hair. Excusing himself, Marosi explained that he would like to talk to the landlady about Eva Szalánczky. The woman eyed the handsome first lieutenant, and clicking along on her stiletto heels, took him to the parlor furnished with overstuffed chairs.

"A little something to drink?" she asked, smiling at Marosi. She returned not only with liquor and little salty cakes, but she had also taken the time to hide her curlers under a red silk scarf. She took a cigarette from Marosi, sat down in one of her chairs, and crossed her stubby thighs in a fashion which made her robe gape open.

"Yes, I heard from the police about Eva's terrible misfortune." The forced solemnity did not fit with her cheeky face. "Poor Evi, who would have thought? . . . I was questioned about who came to see her, and whether she received mail from abroad. They searched her room. Of course, in the concierge's and my presence, but they did not find what they were looking for." She looked at Marosi curiously: "Do they think she was an informer?"

Since he was wearing a uniform, the first lieutenant spoked in an official manner: "It's our duty to uncover everything regarding illegal acts. Discovering the motive in an individual case increases our social awareness."

The woman's vacant look made him change his tone

quickly: "When did Eva Szalánczky move in with you?"

"In 1955." The woman became chipper; she was back in her element. "Eva had just finished her university studies and had started her job at the newspaper. Until then she had lived in a student dormitory, since she didn't have money to rent a room."

She only stayed in the dormitory occasionally, Marosi thought. *Only a few days or weeks between rented rooms.* Eva despised that kind of living, too many people, the shared bedrooms and common baths. Like a bad marriage, she once tried to explain to him, communal living produced problems one could only tolerate briefly.

"How did you two get along?" Marosi wanted to know.

"Perfectly. We hardly ever ran into each other." The woman picked up her glass with the yellow, thick drink and raised it. "Please have some. It's my mother's recipe." She sipped the liquor. "After divorcing my husband, I took in roomers. My child was small and, working for an insurance company, I didn't earn enough. I'm a bookkeeper . . . Well, I have had my experiences with roomers." She smiled contemptuously. "If I rented to a man, he was after me sooner or later. At night, when I had to go to the bathroom, he would wait for me in the hall . . . Well—and a woman is always in my way, cooking, washing and ironing. At night, she tries to sneak her guys into the room. But Evi . . ." The woman was trying to figure out how to present Eva in a positive light. "Evi was a smart woman. She wasn't born a lady, but she sure had turned into one. I woke her in the morning before leaving the house. She had asked me to knock on her door every day. She called 'Yes' and 'Thank You.' She never came home before the concierge locked the front door for the night. We had decided that she would do her láundry on Saturday morning—her day off from work. That way, we wouldn't be in each other's way while doing our chores. She was a very decent human being . . . She often went to the province."

"Who came to see her?" asked Marosi.

The woman became nervous, and sighed: "I don't know. By the time she returned home, I was already asleep. But according to the concierge, she often returned—how shall I say this?—tipsy . . . Often another woman held her up. It wasn't always the same woman; no, it was always a different one. She would say: 'Don't be angry, dear concierge, I'm bringing my friend home, she doesn't feel well.' Well, the one who brought her home stayed here until the next morning. For quite a while I didn't pay any attention to it. These two rooms," she pointed around her, "were locked, and nothing was ever missing from the kitchen, the pantry or the bath—which were unlocked. Not a bit of tea, not even a crumb. I didn't think she was picking up women in the streets as the concierge maintained. Do you realize, officer, how evil people can be? From time to time, I said something to her, but she claimed that there were no more trams, and she thought that her girlfriend, who lived very far away, could sleep on her chaise lounge covered with a coat. Well, that's what she did."

"She didn't have any male visitors?"

"Yes, occasionally men came by, but she was never home."

"Was there anyone who came more than once?"

"Yes." The woman smiled as if thinking of something nice. "All these years he used to come . . . almost always in vain. He was of medium height and rather stocky. A handsome boy. He always arrived with presents—wine, oranges, sardines, chocolate. Once, Evi was in bed with the flu. I didn't dare let him in, and I told him that I had to check if Evi was at home. Evi—with a compress around her neck—whispered hoarsely: 'Tell him, Ilonka, that I'm not here. But he should leave the package.' I felt so sorry for that poor boy . . ."

And consoled him, Marosi thought.

Could I take a look at her room? Or is someone else living there?"

"No, nobody lives there. She paid this month's rent." The woman went ahead down the hall and opened the door to the maid's room. The room was bigger than Marosi had expected, and a bit tube-like. On the wall opposite the door was a white iron bed with a blank mattress. At the end of the bed, a chaise lounge. Along one wall, there was a bedside table, a wash stand, a mirror and a square table; on the opposite wall, there was a big wardrobe, and a small, old-fashioned bookcase. The only window faced the fire wall of the neighboring house. Marosi looked at the bleak room with a heavy heart. No, it would be impossible to return to this room before the front door was locked.

"On Saturday, her brother came here," the woman said. "A decent man. He took her things. Evi only had one suitcase and not everything fit into it. We had to ask the concierge for a paper bag."

The woman squatted and tried to pull out the bottom drawer of the wardrobe. Marosi elbowed her aside and, with some difficulty, pulled out the drawer. It was filled to the brim with paper. The man's heart started beating faster, the same way it had fifteen years ago, when he first set foot into the reading room of a library and had seen the sheer number of books there.

"He left that. I helped him look through everything. We saw these were notes from her studies. What else could we have done with them? I've already thrown a big pile in the garbage can."

"Can I take this with me?" Marosi asked with practiced indifference masking his interest in this treasure. "I think I could make some use of it."

"But of course! At least I won't have to take it out to the trash. Do you know how heavy paper is?" Marosi borrowed a bag from the woman and quickly said good-bye, vowing to return the bag tomorrow or the day after.

5

First Lieutenant Marosi knew the lousy beige paper. Students used it for their notes in the early fifties due to a lack of quality notebooks. After listening to Cunika's idle chatter about the smell of the theater, the limelight, the pleasure of endless applause—even though he didn't know those she gossiped about—and after emptying the bottle of cognac he'd opened that afternoon, he undressed the slightly tipsy woman, helped her into her nightgown, and made his bed on the dining room couch. Then he opened the zipper of the shabby bag and took out the first batch of notes.

"Dialectical and historical materialism. 1954."

Blue ink, energetic, clear script, an exceptionally well-organized outline, with underlined titles, indented subtitles, circled numbers, connecting and separating arrows. Notes on lectures and assigned readings. Marosi visualized the girl in the lecture hall, or in the familiar light of the reading lamp in the Library of Party History. Slowly he leafed through the notes, skimming each page, hoping that the handwriting would alert him of something more interesting than lecture notes. *Oops!*

"THE LAW: Expression of essential, interrelatedness
of phenomena.
I don't care about vanished kisses, old treasures
of a landscape from a fairy tale!
What makes me sad is that
I can give up nothing
that pains me.

LEGALITY: Cause and effect of such connections of phenomena, determining the course of events as given, natural necessity."

The few lines of poetry weren't bad, Marosi thought. Only later did he realize that the person who wrote them must have been quite disturbed emotionally. He continued reading.

"DEVELOPMENT EQUALS THE STRUGGLE OF CONTRADICTIONS
In short: Connections of contradictions (Lenin).
Within me, layers of pain
frozen to ice,
I look at my strong hands:
Why can't the idle worker
grind herself
and be dust?
RECOGNITION OF CONTRADICTIONS OF DEVELOPMENT AS METHOD DIVIDE . . ."

On many pages, nothing but lecture notes. Until Marosi found a longer text at the beginning of an excerpt from Engel's *Origin of the Family, Private Property and the State*:

"I wasn't born a winner. I wasn't born a loser either. I was born a victim.

"I was born a victim in the form of a skinny, anemic baby weighing almost three kilos. Incapable of life, I experienced severe cramps and lost all my color a few days after birth. Everyone used to say I 'wanted to die.' One day, my family—peasants blessed with an exaggerated sense of reality—were getting ready to sit down for their Sunday dinner, after having washed and put on their light summer Sunday dresses. The blood-red meat soup was already steaming on the polished walnut table, when I started—please try to imagine it—preparing for my little infant death. I was lying in my wide, square wicker basket, which had been passed down in my family from one generation to the next. Even as a baby, I was egotistical and badly mannered. My family wasn't very impressed, and I was put in the shed at the end of the house. They thought—and even said among themselves—'If she wants to die, she can very well die, but not during dinner and not in front of us!' I should spare their appetites, after all it was Sunday's dinner, and Sunday dinner only comes once a week. So I was put in the shed. There I lost all interest in dying, and when my mother came looking for me once dinner was finished, I had regained my natural color and demanded my meal with furious screams.

"Later, I often wanted to die. And, again, I was put into the shed, because nobody wanted to lose their appetite, but then nobody came to look after me after their meal was finished."

Marosi sighed, and continued to flip slowly through the notes. Under the headline: "Recognition of the world and its laws," he found the following lines:

"I neither avoid you
nor seek you out,
I simply endure the day
I met you.
You look through me
as through glass,
I look through you
and my eyes bleed.
Once, I would like to ask:
Don't you ever suffer?"

When the first lieutenant came to the end of the pile of notes, he was sorry that there were no more. He took the four pages which interested him, tossed the rest into Cunika's garbage can and turned off the light.

6

W hen Marosi double checked with the hospital's doorman if the information provided by Livia's sister was correct, the name Livia Kismányoki wasn't found. But when the first lieutenant mentioned that he was looking for a young woman who had been shot by her husband, the old doorman understood.

"You want Ödön Horváth's wife. Yes, that's correct. Surgical ward, second floor, room fourteen."

It was nine o'clock. Marosi had chosen that time, knowing that the morning routine would be over, but the hospital rounds would not have started. Mrs. Ödön Horváth. He pondered the unsympathetic sounding name. What kind of mother would baptize her newborn with the old-fashioned name Ödön?

There were six beds in the room, and Marosi felt the eyes of six women on him. He was confused. He went along the ends of the beds, glanced at the charts, and barely deciphered the names. He was already in front of the last bed next to the window, when he suddenly stepped back and then leaned slightly forward: Mrs. Ödön Horváth.

An attentive, sad look met his. Her eyes were her most prominent feature. The face itself was pale, the perfect proportions—her small nose, full lips—reminding him of a Greek statue. The golden hair was spread over the graying pillow case, and above the blue nightgown, rose a neck without wrinkles. So much beauty caused almost physical pain in Marosi—nevertheless, his eyes remained fixed on the big, mysterious eyes shining under heavy eyelids, which, like reflectors, gave this face a special light.

"Livia Kismányoki?" he asked, embarrassed.

"Yes," said the woman.

"I'm First Lieutenant Marosi."

The woman closed her eyes, then opened, and said with tired resignation: "Take a chair and sit down."

Marosi did as he was told. The patient in the next bed, an old woman who had been staring curiously, bashfully turned away.

"What do you still want from me?" Livia asked, tormented. "I've already told everything to Major Blindics."

Blindics. Major Blindics, Marosi thought, *I have to remember that name. Blindics.*

"Excuse me," he said with a smile, "I'm not a cop. I'm a soldier. I'm here because of Eva Szalánczky."

The patient eyed the handsome man contemptuously, as if to say: *Who are you really talking about? Me or Eva?*

"I've asked Eva to leave me alone," she spoke very softly. "I asked her not to come and see me, nor to bring any more books, nor flowers, and not to write any letters. I asked her emphatically to get out of my life. I had hoped that she had listened, because I haven't heard from her in two weeks . . . And now *you* are here."

Marosi looked at her closely.

"Why are you so angry with her?"

"Listen," Livia said, with flashing eyes. She tried to sit up, but fell back. "I'm twenty-seven, and one of my legs might remain paralyzed for the rest of my life. I, whose fate it was . . ." she grimaced, ". . . *supposedly* to carry a beautiful body on beautiful legs, will remain lame. Do you know the saying that everybody lives off what they have the most of? I've lived off my beauty . . . At least that's what she said . . . And now it's possible that I will remain lame . . . With a little bit of good will, Eva could have prevented that fateful shot. And I shouldn't be angry with her?"

"I would think that she could not have prevented it," Marosi said carefully.

"She could have." She talked softly, but with glowing excitement. "When we parted, when Ödön took her to the bus stop, he told her very clearly that he wanted to kill me. 'During the night, I'll kill that carcass,' he said. She jumped on the bus and called back: 'Whoever hurts Livia will have to deal with me!' Then she went back home and slept, instead—"

"What could she have done?

"She could have called me. To warn me. It would not have been the first time I took my child to spend the night at my mother's."

She has a child, thought Marosi.

"Or I could have stayed up all night, I could have resisted sleep to avoid being killed. He's such a mad dog! No, she went home and went to sleep peacefully."

"She didn't take your husband's threats seriously," Marosi offered cautiously.

"That's her excuse," Livia declined. "I have no proof to the contrary . . . I feel that she didn't want to take him seriously, didn't want to prevent my murder, because in the depths of her soul she wanted me dead. She herself had played with the idea of killing me."

Marosi was deeply shocked.

"What would have been her reason for that?"

Surprise prevented Livia from answering. Anger and spite churned inside her, and her words were filled with measured emotion: "You tell me that Eva sent you here! And she would not have told you that? . . ." Suddenly she looked at Marosi: "Who *are* you? What do you want from me?"

"Eva never talked about me?" He tried to smile engagingly. "She didn't tell you about the military engineer?"

"What do I know? We talked about many things," the woman said impatiently. "In one and a half years, one talks about many things. But please, tell me: What do you want from me?"

A pretty and fresh-looking nurse appeared in the doorway: "My dears! Put on your most beautiful robes! Do your hair! Smile! The doctors will come soon!" She looked at Marosi, and approached him with a polite smile: "Would you be so kind as to stop this interrogation! Poor thing, when will she be left in peace?"

The nurse thinks I'm a detective, Marosi thought. He got up and asked Livia softly: "When can I come back?"

"Never, *ever*," the woman said vehemently. "Don't come back! I don't want the past thrown in my face. I don't want to see Eva Szalánczky."

"I have some information which might be of interest to you," Marosi volunteered.

"I'm not interested."

"Eva Szalánczky is dead."

Marosi watched all the blood drain from the angry face. Perhaps the full, trembling lips said soundlessly: "No, that's not true!"

Marosi bowed and left the hospital room.

7

F erenc Erdös received Marosi promptly, as soon as his
secretary told him that Marosi had come to discuss
the case of Eva Szalánczky. Erdös was a small, seemingly
ascetic man, with a considerably sized head on rather nar-
row shoulders. His mighty nose was boldly bent down-
ward, and he wore a petrified, bitter smile on his thin,
bloodless lips. He looked soberly at the world.

There was a conference table in his shabby office;
nevertheless, after shaking hands with Marosi, Erdös asked
him to sit down on a chair opposite his desk. Erdös also
sat down. On the desk, in the middle of a terrible clutter
of manuscripts, newspapers, galleys, photographs and reports, there was a small, clear space, in which Erdös kept
the pieces of a dismantled pipe. Ferenc Erdös cleaned the
pipe stem with cut-up envelopes, paper-clips and cotton
batting.

As Eva Szalánczky's editor, Erdös had already officially
been informed of her death. After a few moments of chit-
chat, he declared: "We are responsible for her death. Directly, as well as indirectly. We sent her to Mohács on a
story. That is, we suggested it to her, and she agreed . . .
Who would have thought such a thing would happen?"

"How long did you know Eva Szalánczky, Comrade
Erdös?"

Engrossed, the editor-in-chief cleaned his pipe. He blew
through the short, straight shaft.

"I'll have to begin in 1951, during the second wave of

the Rajk trials, when I was arrested. I'm a journalist, and I had joined the Party at the beginning. From 1947 on, I held an important position in the COMINFORM. I had my own little group, to some degree in opposition to the majority position. We used to be the Erdös faction. I'm sure you have never heard of us."

"No," Marosi confessed.

"In 1955, we were rehabilitated. We were called to the appropriate office, where we were given a few thousand forints and asked where we would like to work. I was disgusted with politics, and I retreated to an archive. After 1956, I saw, once again, that the political tide was changing. When I was asked again—this time, not by those who had put me into jail, but by those with whom I had spent time in jail—if I wouldn't like to return to my former profession, I asked to be assigned to a newspaper as editor-in-chief.

"We began publishing *People and Culture* on the first of January of last year. I did not choose most of my co-workers; they were sent to me by the Party. Generally, I'm satisfied with them . . . As it is with new papers, writers interested in contributing show up frequently. A few months after we started, I received a letter which caught my attention. It differed greatly from letters I normally receive. The writer was clearly an engaged person expressing her own thoughts and opinions. It was Eva Szalánczky. Who is this woman? I wondered. I only knew that she was a young journalist. I asked her to come and see me. A starveling—excuse the expression—showed up in my office. Her dress was worn out, her face was thin, her eyes greedy. She made me think of the Budapest saying: 'I'm hungry. I'm thirsty. I'm tired. I'm cold and I need to *piss*.' She drank her coffee in small gulps, and she smoked her cigarette all the way to the end of the butt.

"'You don't have a job?' I asked her.

"'That's the case.'

"'How long have you been out of work?'

"'Since January first, 1957, when our newspaper was closed down.'

"You know," the editor-in-chief turned to Marosi, "that all the newspapers were closed down, in order to re-organize them under the authority of responsible Party cadre. A day later, the newspapers appeared again, staffed mostly by the old guard because there was nobody else left."

Erdös screwed his pipe together.

"What do we say? 'We have no choice; we've only got the riffraff.'" He took aromatic tobacco out of his leather pouch and stuffed it into the pipe. "I also asked Eva if she had had another job since then.

"'No,' she said.

"'And why not?'

"'I don't know.'

"'Did you give them any reason not to hire you?'

"'No.'

"'What did you do in 1956?'

"'Nothing.'

"'You didn't do anything?'

"'I was waiting. I didn't understand what was going on; it was all too much for me. I wasn't compelled to be on either side. I was waiting. Like the peasants. Waiting. What would come next . . .'

"'How do you explain, then, that you didn't get another job?'

"'Look, Comrade Erdös,' she said . . ."

The editor-in-chief put the pipe in his mouth, lit it and puffed until it was working, then took it out of his mouth . . . "Eva said to me: 'I came to Budapest at the age of twenty. I was a student and I didn't know a single soul. I used to be an excellent student, my classmates liked me and they looked up to me as a role model. I really believed

47

a new class of intellectuals—coming from the people—was in the making. After the government examination, I was supposed to choose where I wanted to work. I wanted to be a journalist, and it was clear that I would get a job with a newspaper. But when . . .'" the editor-in-chief puffed on his pipe, "'. . . my job was abolished due to some administrative order, nobody paid any attention to me. My acquaintances preferred to cross the streets illegally, straight into the arms of a cop, who would fine them ten forints, simply to avoid talking to me. They did not want to be compromised by me. I went to the university office for some help—after all, I had studied there for five years; they knew my accomplishments and they knew that I used to be a tutor. But they sent me away, telling me that they were only responsible for their current students. My former teachers defended their powerlessness, and also sent me away to protect their reputations . . . In short, Comrade Erdös,' Eva Szalánczky said, '. . . I discovered that we were hardly in the process of educating a new people's intelligentsia, that we hadn't buried the old intelligentsia, and that any claim to the contrary was utter bullshit. Yes, we all went to peoples' universities in those days, but the songs we sang, like "Glowing Winds," were meaningless. You can't force people to believe even song lyrics, so they all just sang along, smiling hypocritically. *Smelly peasant go back to work in the fields!* That's why I didn't get another job after 1956.'

"'And you?' I asked her. 'What do you think about this new and bitter experience?'"

Erdös puffed on his pipe with great pleasure and then he continued: "Eva looked me in the eye, and said something which made me fall for her: 'This country is *my* country, whether you like it or not.'"

The editor-in-chief was silent; the smile in the turned down corners of his mouth even more bitter: "Well, this country wasn't her country after all!" He looked at Marosi. "I hired her immediately. I couldn't give her permanent employment, only free-lance work. I was warned. Even by my superiors. They said that I should not compromise myself with the 'appearance of such a suspicious element.' They couldn't tell me anything concrete; they only knew that Eva Szalánczky had been connected to certain 1956 trials . . . As a witness. That was enough to conclude that some of her friends and acquaintances had gone to jail, and others had gone abroad."

This explains the odd responses to my questions when I called all those phone numbers in her address book, Marosi thought.

Thoughtfully, Erdös puffed on his pipe.

"When the actress Katalin Karády fled Hungary, forty-two people were arrested. Among them, her pedicurist, who had done nothing but her feet once a week. I don't think you can classify that as 'desertion.' True, it occurred during the darkest moments of the Rákosi era. Should we start all over again with the trials, purges, etc.? Is someone deserving of suspicion if he knew the deputy of defense minister Maleter, at a time when he wasn't even Maleter's deputy, but just a young man who was courting Eva? If someone breaks into my neighbor's flat, and if they ask me if I have seen anything, do I become as much a suspect as the burglar? A strange European way of thinking. According to Anglo-Saxon law, everybody is considered innocent until proven guilty. One prefers to set free ninety-nine guilty ones, rather than allow one innocent person to suffer. After the American War of Independence, the defeated generals were not imprisoned—only one person was punished, the commander of a prisoner of war camp, but only because he was a sadist and had tortured the inmates. In the spirit of this system, Churchill disapproved of the Nuremberg Trials. He wrote that if the British had lost the war, they'd be facing the gallows now. Grass grows over battlefields, but never under gallows . . . Here, it's different, we apply Roman law with its drastic measures. Everybody is guilty, unless he can prove his innocence. Terrible, no? Would you like to have a coffee?"

"Yes, thanks," said Marosi. The editor-in-chief called his secretary and asked for a coffee.

"I asked Szalánczky in which district and for which section of the paper she would like to work. She wanted to do investigative reporting. I was very pleased with this, because we didn't have enough people—even today we are short. During the Rákosi era, writers and journalists gave up on the empirical study of the truth . . . You might remember that famous nonsense: 'The eye is not only the tool, but the barrier to our vision.' News stories were classified as merely 'natural' (even the bourgeois can manage empiricism) and not 'realistic,' which requires the political interpretation of the Party. In the particular case of news reporting, naturalism got in the way of realism. The journalists didn't know anything about life, and therefore had no way of uncovering the truth about life. Every factory worker and Party secretary misled them, according to his own beliefs. The journalists had no experience behind them to expose such bias. And, at the same time, there was an atmosphere of uneasiness. Subordinates didn't dare talk; higher-ranking employees turned the most unimportant information into state secrets. In short, our reporters were reporting only the most superficial trivia. They were incapable of grasping the essence . . . In the investigative section, I needed new people."

"Who else was working there?" Marosi wanted to know.

"Livia Kismányoki was the department head," said Erdös, and knocked his pipe against the heavy glass ash tray. "And then there were two young journalists, Agnes Rusák and Attila Hagymási."

Marosi stored these two names in his memory.

"Once a week, we have an editorial meeting, and every-body can talk about their general ideas regarding the paper as a whole, or concerns specific to their section. I thought that I would have to suggest story ideas to Eva Szalánczky, at least at the beginning. But she didn't need my help; even at her first editorial meeting, she came up with brilliant ideas. All the old writers grew pale with jealousy. 'The little one is a bit too zealous,' my assistant said, and laughed vulgarly. 'She believes—she thinks she can prove—that anything can be done here. The prevailing atmosphere will take her pleasure away. Within six months, she'll be as phlegmatic, cross and weak-willed as the rest of us.' You know," Erdös went on explaining, "the atmosphere after 1956 didn't help much in our work. The intellectuals were pretty helpless; we knew that something was gone, but we didn't know what would come in its place. Some feared, and others hoped, that everything would continue the way it used to be before 1956. Of course, there were a few who hoped that a totally different solution would be applied, but they had no idea what it would be like. The atmosphere in the editor's office was very bad. I only became aware of it after Szalánczky had written her first stories. Only by reflecting on her stories, did I become aware of the unbear-able schemes and boring items which filled the paper's columns. I don't want to exaggerate, but every one of Eva Szalánczky's lines was a sensation . . ."

Marosi resolved to read these articles.

". . . unfortunately, such a sensation that her stories were unpublishable," the editor-in-chief continued regretfully. "This would have meant tempting the gods, and we would have paid for it with our lives—Eva's and mine. Of course," Erdös again played with his pipe, "mine would not have mattered, I would have returned to the archive. But I couldn't allow a young person's life to be destroyed. In her own interest, I didn't publish those provocative articles.

She questioned our politics—no matter what she wrote. In vain, I assigned her the most harmless stories, but under her pen they turned into something that I couldn't publish. For example, she wrote about a cultural center on the city's outskirts, claiming that it wasn't a house of culture, but a tavern. She claimed that the child care centers didn't provide a service to society, but only served to cover up the lack of women's equality. And so on. Once, she suggested a series of reports about the events of 1956 in the countryside. She wanted to document what happened in October 1956 in various villages. I gave her my blessings. She spent two months in the villages, and returned with ten stories. Excellent writing, but not for publication. She proved that the policies implemented during the Rákosi era—among them, his agrarian policies directed against the peasants and his unpopular policies favoring Party members—had led to the counter-revolution. And to top it off, she thought that the counter-revolutionaries' demand for power in 1956 was actually a revolution. Not taking into consideration that the people would have fought the counter-revolutionaries under any circumstance . . . She had a beautiful and clever way of describing this phenomenon . . ." Again Erdös filled his pipe, mulling. "'The storm stirs up the dirt, but it also sweeps it away.' . . . Now, dear Marosi, to defend the erroneous point of view that a revolution took place in Hungary in 1956 is enough to count as conspiracy, and conspiracy takes you straight to jail . . . Believe me, I was in a difficult position. As editor-in-chief, as well as an individual."

The phone on his desk rang. He picked it up, annoyed with the disturbance, and said almost rudely: "Later!" before hanging up.

"I observed how she developed from a hungry prairie dog into a well-dressed, quite secure young woman thanks to regular pay. After each pay day, she appeared prettier. A new suit, a new bag, new shoes, a dazzling white blouse. If you ask me, I think she sacrificed her food to pay her tailor. But in stark contrast to her increasingly positive appearance, she became—as I also observed—increasingly despondent, lethargic, antisocial, lonelier and more and more hopeless. I believe that everyone in the editor's office liked her. But everyone also considered her to be a tragic visionary who ran full tilt at everything . . ." He looked at Marosi. "Do you know the saying, 'Whether the stone hits the egg, or the egg the stone, it doesn't matter, because in any case, the egg breaks . . .'? Well, it was clear that nobody but Eva would break. I tried to help her. I gave her book reviews. She had studied literature, and it should have been easy for her. And indeed, she was very capable! She wrote that our approved, highly praised writers, were untruthful and insignificant. About young, government-loyal careerists, she wrote openly that they were careerists who didn't have the faintest notions about life. She put me, the editor-in-chief, in an increasingly difficult situation. For months, I paid a contributor from whom we were only allowed to publish a few articles. 'Didn't we tell you?' said those triumphant ones who had predicted it." Erdös lit his pipe and puffed on it for a long time. "And despite all this, I couldn't send her away. It was she who resigned. Maybe she was afraid to carry things too far. That was four months ago."

"How did she justify her resignation?" Marosi asked.

"That she couldn't bear it any longer."

"She gave no explanation that involved another person?"

"As far as I know, no. She was a very inaccessible human being."

"What were her plans?"

"That's what I asked her, too," said the editor-in-chief. "But she had no plans. Nothing whatsoever; she only told me that she wanted to go back to her village. I assured her that whenever she would bring me an article, of course, one that could be used . . . and now . . . the notice of death."

The silence was interrupted by the ringing phone. Erdös picked it up. "Just a bit more patience," he said and hung up again.

"Could I take a look at those stories about the villages?" asked Marosi while getting up.

"Unfortunately not, our only copies went to . . . Well our superiors have asked for them," said Erdös with a regretful voice. He also had gotten up. "If you really want to see them, then I'll try to get them back. How long are you going to stay in Budapest?"

"A few more days," said Marosi, while he stretched out his hand to Erdös. "Many thanks for your kindness, Comrade Editor-in-Chief. With your permission, I'll call on you again."

8

I n the middle of Eva's papers, Marosi found an almost empty notebook. Eva had only written a few pages: "I planned to spend Christmas at home with my parents, but L. told me that she would like to celebrate my patron saint's day on December 24. So far I've spent every Christmas at home, because there is nothing more awful than spending the holidays in a rented room, furnished with little but despair . . . The pubs close at eight, nine, ten, and then the city is dead. The streets are empty, and only in the windows can one see the glow of lit up Christmas trees. But only strangers live behind these windows. And everyone is a stranger.

"I didn't have any particular desire to go home this year. Since I left home in 1950, their complaints haven't changed: suffering, disease, taxes, lack of money, the village chairperson, the producers' co-operative—they are all so involved in their own troubles. Not once in the last eight years has anyone bothered to ask: 'Evi, how are you?' Not once! On top of it, I didn't have any money, at least not what I needed to cover a Christmas at home. There are so many nieces and nephews, and if I bought only a chocolate bar or a book for each, I would need at least five hundred forints. I just spent two thousand at my tailor's for a new winter coat and one thousand at my shoemaker's for a pair of boots. My god, for eight years I haven't had a new winter coat, and I've spent my whole life with freezing feet, because I never owned more than one pair of shoes, which were soaking wet by October and never dried until May. I went to school the whole winter with drenched shoes and my feet were always itching from water mites. What does this mean? How does medicine define this scourge of the poor? The feet itch so badly that one would like to scratch not only the skin, but peel off the flesh as well. The only thing that helps is to warm your feet in the oven. Everybody at home had this problem, and, according to age, we took turns warming our feet. After nine o'clock, we let the fire die out, and since my turn came only then, there was little warmth left. Well, I ordered a pair of fur-lined boots for a thousand forints, because I had decided that never again did I want to have frozen feet. So I had no money to go home for Christmas. It would have been possible to borrow some, but I didn't even think about it, because L.'s invitation made me hot. Six o'clock, eight o'clock, at ten o'clock the latest, L. would go home, and I would be left alone, unhappy as a screaming prairie wolf in a ghastly Hungarian night. But, I thought, even *that* was worth it.

"The day before Christmas, on December 23, we left the editor's office at four-thirty. There were four of us. H. and R. came along. We went to an espresso. At that time, I didn't know the street it was on, nor its name, even though I had been there a few times. But now I know, it's called Cinea; I've remembered its name in the meantime. The room is L-shaped. One enters at the 'foot' of the L and immediately faces the counter with the coffee machine and a row of tables. The front wall is a window which, at night, reflects the whole room. I only noticed *this* after Christmas.

"When we sat down, I said immediately that I had no money.

"'Just relax,' said H. 'It's your patron saint's day. Don't bother with anything.'

"We drank cognac. Slowly people emptied out of the espresso. R. and H. exchanged suggestive glances, and then H. asked if we wanted to stay. 'We'll stay a bit,' said L. H. paid the bill and, as a pretense, he asked me to come to the coat room. With a chummy smile under his thin mustache, he slipped me a hundred forint bill. 'If you want to, you can return it, but it doesn't matter if you don't. In any case, I support you.'

"The waitress came to L. and me, and asked if we wanted anything else. We ordered two cognacs. All the other customers had left, even though the espresso wouldn't close for another hour.

"'I would like to kiss your hand,' I said.

"L. offered me her mouth.

"I was watching out for the waitress. Since we were sitting in the far corner of the room, our table could not be seen from the front counter.

"'Come home with me,' I begged L.

"'Quiet. Let me have your mouth again. You have a beautiful mouth. Where did you get such a beautiful mouth?'

"I didn't dare lose my head. I kept an eye on the front of the espresso to see if the waitress was coming back. I glanced at my watch. Ten minutes before closing time. I tore myself away and called for the bill. The waitress appeared with a sly smile, but it was not offensive. I paid and gave her a big tip.

"We went out into the street. It was very cold, at least twenty degrees below zero. I wanted to walk along the boulevards circling the city's center. L. took my hand and led me in the opposite direction. We entered a snow-covered park. L. swept frozen snow from the first bench and sat down. Only later did I notice the street light right above us. L. pulled me toward her and we continued our love play.

"'Come to my room,' I implored. 'Trust me, I won't do any more than you want.'

"'I'll come some day,' panted L.

"'When?'

"'I don't know. I don't know yet.'

"Occasionally, a pedestrian hastened by, looked at us with mild surprise, and continued on his way.

"'Come to me,' I pleaded.

"'Sometime.'

"'When?'

"'Don't talk now. I adore your mouth. It is a soft, single pleading, but still it has so much more power than I have ever encountered.'

"'I love you,' I said. 'Come to me.'

"'I'll come one day.'

"'I'm inhibited and I am vain. And I'm proud of the fact that no one has ever pushed my caressing hand away. I just don't let myself get carried away to the point where someone would have to humiliate me like that. I'd hate anyone who did that. Sitting on that bench, I lost my head. I started to touch L.'s ankle bone, and as I didn't feel any resistance, my hand moved up higher between her thighs.

"'Terrible . . .' L. sighed.

"'Terribly bad?' I asked.

"'Terribly good.'

"At that moment we heard a harsh voice: 'Your papers please!'

"We stopped hugging. I looked around me. Four cops had encircled us. We handed over our papers and they examined them carefully. One of the cops, apparently the superior officer, must have weighed at least a hundred kilos. He said to L.:

"'You are married. Why do you put yourself in such a position?'

"'That's my business,' said L. defiantly. But I could see the effect this question had on her.

"'If we catch you again, we'll report you to your editor's office and we'll tell your husband. Understood?' He returned L.'s papers. 'Go home now.'

"She left without saying a word. She lives in one of the housing projects on the outskirts of the city. I looked after her. 'My god,' I thought, 'how is she going to get home? Will she find a cab?'

"'You'll come with us,' the cop said to me, after having

put my papers in his pocket.

"I got into their car. When we drove off, one of them said half cynically, half enviously:

"'We watched you for two hours. I've never seen such passion, and I'm from the vice squad. Must be a great love?'

"'My dear man,' I said while the car was speeding to the headquarters on Deák Street, 'for someone working with the vice squad, you are pretty naïve. If this was a great love, the two of us wouldn't be kissing in a park at twenty degrees below zero. We'd be in our own flat, or in a flat which we might borrow for the occasion. I have a room— I'm a boarder—but she didn't want to come home with me. She only wanted to kiss in the park. That's not love.' Full of bitterness, I added: 'She won't come back. You really scared her, and you have really spoiled my pleasure.'

"We stopped in front of headquarters. One of the cops disappeared inside with my papers in his hand. Ten minutes later, he returned.

"'Go home,' he said and gave me my papers back. 'You are hopeless.'

"I didn't move.

"'Gentlemen,' I said, 'since you already screwed up my evening, I would like you to take me someplace where I can get something to drink. What is still open?'

"They took me to the bar of a first-class hotel and we said cordial good-byes.

"I spent the holidays sleeping and doing laundry, alternating between despair and hope. There were two surprises waiting for me on my first day back at work. The first: L. had exchanged desks with A. I found out in the morning, when I tumbled into the editor's office. She had moved to the office next door. I called her:

"'What's the matter?' I asked.

"'I'm afraid of you,' she said. 'I don't want to destroy my life.'

"'What kind of fidelity has to be protected by walls?' I

asked. 'Are you wearing a chastity belt? I can't rape you. Nothing can happen between us, except what you also desire.'

"'I'm afraid of myself,' she said on the phone. 'You offer me a life of tragedy, which moves me and makes me defenseless. At the same time I'm repulsed, because I feel that you are pulling me into some kind of abyss. I really must ask you to leave me alone.'

"'You ask *me* to leave *you* alone? Why did you start then?'

"'It doesn't matter who started it,' she said and hung up.

"I dialed again.

"'And of course it matters,' I said as soon as I heard her voice, 'because whoever started it carries a greater responsibility. Even though she might not want to shoulder that responsibility.'

"Again she hung up the phone, again I dialed.

"'Nobody forced you to show love. Nobody forced you to show anything you didn't feel. In the working class suburb where you were born, people pick up knives for less. Don't you know that?'

"She slammed down the phone and didn't answer again. I began my work day by dictating a story. I took it to her office and left it on her desk without a word. She looked at me briefly. Scared. H., who was sitting at the other desk, must have seen something, because he jumped up and followed me into the hall.

"'Is something the matter?' he asked with real concern.

"'Nothing,' I refused to tell him anything. 'I have a headache. I drank too much last night.'

"'Everybody is drinking too much,' he said. 'If you want to, we could continue together tonight.'

"'You are sweet,' I said and left him. I really don't want to talk with him. The last bit of my joy in living would disappear. A disappointed human being, cynical and without will power. In 1956, I returned from an assignment in the province and told him that Zala county collectives were still organized with billy clubs. He said: 'But now we have the producers' co-operatives, you can't beat *that* with a rubber stick.'

"At noon, we had a short meeting, and then I went to have lunch in the canteen with A. She invited me to go to the movies with her, but I wanted to talk to L. at any price. Repeatedly, I had called her that morning, but every time she slammed down the phone once she recognized my voice. Later, when I went to the bathroom, I saw a small, inert officer pick her up. They left together.

"It seemed as if my world was breaking down. It wasn't pain, I only felt incredible anger and contempt. The meaner someone is, the more humiliating her rejection.

"The weather had warmed up, and the slush in the city was ankle-deep. It seemed as if I was wading through snot and tears, and my insides were washed away like the river banks after a flood. Something forced me to walk in the direction of my saint's day espresso. When I entered, the employees seemed to be smirking at me. I stood near the counter, and as I looked around for an empty table, my glance wandered to the front wall. In the darkness of the window, one could see the whole room as clearly as in a big mirror. Even the furthest corner table, where we had kissed. That's why the waitress didn't show up for nearly an hour. Free of charge, all the employees had been the audience to our performance. With a burning face, I sneaked out like a beaten dog. I wouldn't dare ever return to this place.

"At the moment, I'm sitting in another espresso. It will close very soon, and I don't know what to do.

"I'll write another Christmas card to my family, dated the twentieth. Julius Fučik wrote from death row: 'Father! Mother! Why is your son so strong?'—Don't know why this came to mind now."

9

"**D**id you find anything?" asked Cunika, arriving home from the theater at midnight. As her face was still shining with make-up, she bent to hug Marosi, but carefully avoided kissing him.

"Maybe," said Marosi.

Cunika disappeared in the bathroom. Marosi gathered Eva's papers. He had been reading all evening, separating the dry class notes from the diary entries and the few fragmented poems, which he now stacked into a neat pile and placed in a special folder. That afternoon, he had called more of the numbers from Eva's address book, but either no one had picked up the phone, or he was told that the person he was calling had moved away. Five of the names from the address book, he learned, belonged to people who had defected.

Cunika had taken off her make-up and had returned to the living room, wrapped in a bathrobe and smelling sweetly. She took a sip of the cognac which Marosi had bought, and sulking, she noted:

"You are still dressed?"

"That's an old habit, Cunika. I can only work when I'm dressed," Marosi defended himself. "Until I was twenty-six, I never owned a bathrobe or a cardigan. My room wasn't heated, and I wouldn't have survived in just my pajamas. I had to work fully dressed. Even now, as soon as I undress, I relax as if on command, and my thoughts just dissolve."

"You still want to work tonight?" Cunika was taken aback.

"No, I was hoping we could talk."

"Let's talk in bed . . . That's the best place to talk."

"That's true. But it's late, and afterwards we would immediately fall asleep."

Cunika yawned in agreement, picked up her glass and settled herself onto the chair opposite his. They smoked and drank.

"What do you want to talk about?"

"You didn't like Eva Szalánczky, did you?"

"Is it possible to like a role model?" Disdainfully, she pursed her lips.

"Role model. What do you mean by that?"

"In gymnasium she was the 'heroic student,' straight A's, the winner of all study and essay competitions. When we came to Budapest we stayed in touch for another two years, and it was only then that we became friends. You know how terribly lonely a student can be, especially when she comes from the province and doesn't know a single soul in the capital. I often got movie and theater tickets, and if I couldn't find anyone to come along, I took Eva. I thought that she was arrogant. Such a know-it-all. She knew more about the plays we saw—even though *I* had studied them. She was better read, knew more about politics, and she coached me through my Marxism exams, otherwise I would have failed." Cunika smiled bitterly. "Even today I can hear her mocking me: 'You've got to know this, my dear artist.' But I allowed her to treat me like this; I wasn't offended. During my third year, the filmmaker Dunaszegi prepared a film about our 'new industrial city of Sztálinváros,' and he was looking for someone to play a hodwoman. She didn't need to be very pretty, just like a real hodwoman. She couldn't be too ugly either, otherwise it would have been difficult to sell the film. And I was selected."

Cunika filled the two glasses. Her reddened face displayed a certain vulnerability.

"I can talk honestly with you, can't I? You know almost everything about me. I was in love with a guy. He was a student and wanted to be a composer. Neither of us had a flat. We made love in doorways, in the woods on the outskirts of the city, on benches, at the last stop of empty tramways. Afterwards we felt ashamed and fought for days . . .

"Dunaszegi invited me for dinner at the Gellért Hotel, claiming that he needed to talk about my part. I had never been to such an elegant restaurant, had never eaten venison stew, never a pheasant, and never a trout. He showed me which silver to use to eat fish . . . I was dizzy. It hadn't occurred to me that he wanted to be 'paid' for the part. He said that he had rented a room and that I should come up. I believed that he was attracted to me and went along. Half a year later, the film was done, he won a prize, and I was an established actress. It also took exactly half a year for him to get a divorce and to kick his wife out of their flat."

Marosi was about to explain that he wasn't interested in her marriage, but in Eva Szalánczky, but Cunika insisted on finishing her story.

"I moved into the flat and invited all my girlfriends to show off—why should I lie about it? Also to brag to Eva. She was really disgusting. She's always judged everything under the sun, saying, 'I don't care *who* is harmed by the truth, I'm only interested in the truth.' That day, she went too far, though." Cunika filled the glasses, old anger still seething. "I can't repeat the discussion in complete detail, but I still remember the essentials:

"'How old is your husband?' Eva asked me.

"'Forty-five.'

"'Twice your age.'

"'So what?'

"'Do you love him?'

"'Of course.'

"'Who was his first wife?'

"'He has been married twice. Before the war, to the daughter of a brandy distiller and, after 1945, to the daughter of a Party functionary who had returned from Moscow.'

"'Was she Jewish?'

"'I don't know.'

"'But I do. And now he's married to someone from the peoples' cadre, a true working class child. A nice list.'

"'You can't imagine that he loves me?'

"'Why not? You are twenty years younger than his first wife. If he wasn't such a rich filmmaker and owner of this beautiful flat—inherited or possibly distributed by the state—would you have gotten married to him?'

"'Stupid question. His filmmaking, his flat—aren't they part of him? His money—isn't it his?'

"'I'll ask you something else. If Tibi, the music student, had such a beautiful flat, which one would you have married?'

"'Look, the thing with Tibi had already lasted for two years. We were close to breaking up anyway.'

"Then my husband returned home. I introduced the two of them, and it was clear to me that they couldn't stand each other. I was afraid that they might get into a fight, but it didn't happen. Both of them were polite, disciplined people, and they settled for a heated political discussion instead. I have to admit," she smiled at Marosi, "I didn't understand much of it. What I understood was the following: Eva explained to him why his film was bad, just another B-movie. She herself had never worked on a construction site, but in her extended family there were all kinds of workers—factory workers, construction workers, and yes, hodmen and bricklayers—and she often talked with them. Based on these talks, she was in a position to see their problems and have an *honest* understanding—based in reality—of the current situation of the working class.

"According to Eva, there were two oppressed classes, the workers and the peasants. The idyllic picture shown in our film—its title, by the way, was 'Little Veronica'—was a vulgar lie. She said: 'Foremen, Party secretaries, chief engineers would *never* help a hodwoman, a girl from the countryside. They would only try to screw her.

"'Also the picture of the workers' tiled rooms, where people live together harmoniously, was a lie. Women's quarters were furnished with bunk beds, and there was never enough money for curtains in the windows. And in the evenings, and at night, all the lumpen from the city would loll about, waiting to rape girls.

"'There was no hot water in workers' housing, nor was it possible to take a bath or cook a meal. There were no radios—but there *were* always a few thieves. Nobody knows who was stealing, and everybody was suspicious of everyone else. The idyllic marriage with the bricklayer's foreman, the honest stachanovist, was also a lie.

"'Stachanovism is a lie, because the wall built with such absurd methods of production will collapse in six months. A stachanovist is only a tool in the hands of those who want to bring up the quotas of the non-stachanovists, the regular construction workers. The workers just get squeezed one more time.'"

"That's all quite significant," Marosi lifted his glass and toasted Cunika, who almost blushed from such praise.

"In all honesty," she continued, "my father and other relatives said the same things about the film. But they gave me credit for being good in it. Nice, naïve, dewy. I only remember it so well, because I heard it from Eva for the first time. At that time, I was of course very indignant. My husband even more so. I watched his neck turn red . . . Those two marks on his neck . . ." Cunika buried her head in her hands. "At the beginning I didn't mind them. Later, I hated his neck the most. It disgusted me. But by then he

66

was already disgusted with me." She lifted her head, drank more cognac, and her face was placid again.

"This was nothing. I tell you, until that point, it was nothing, only later did she become personal. She insisted that Dunaszegi and people like him—who had grown up in flats with ten thousand books on the shelves, graduated from gymnasium in Vienna and had gone to university in Berlin, who had classical educations at their finger tips, who during their youth had been in contact with the European avant garde—such people could not be so stupid as to sincerely work for the current, lying, scheming cultural establishment. And, she said, if they weren't stupid, then they must have been cynical. Such art can only be produced under two conditions: either one is naïve and believes in the crap he is producing; or, one is cynical and thinks that if stupid politicians need this poor excuse for art—and if this is the only way they'll shell out money, prizes, villas—then the only thing to do is to produce it for them. They'll get what they deserve.

"But the true artist, Eva said, doesn't create art for power or for politicians, but for the people or for artists and other intellectuals. That I can accept. I think, though, she said to Dunaszegi, that you don't know anything about the girl who was dragging plaster in Sztálinváros. If you want, you can film a love story with two, a triangle, or even one with four lovers. You can make a film about the fact that life doesn't make sense. You could also make a film based on some schlocky Courths-Mahler novel. But what obliges you to do something on a topic you know nothing about and in which you are not even interested? Who or what is forcing you to do it? Only your career ambitions! Nothing else. To hell with a people who are betrayed even by their own intellectuals!"

Exhausted, Cunika fell silent. She put her elbows on the table, drew in her pretty shoulders and stared ahead with a hopeless expression on her face. Marosi leaned over the table, and tenderly stroked her hair.

"Don't be angry . . ."

"I think Eva was right . . . About everything . . . I remember another of her sayings: 'Make a compromise only once. Only once. How much does it cost? . . . Everything. Compromises are like runs in a stocking. They keep on running, and in the end the person is just one big run.'"

"Don't be bitter," Marosi whispered, embracing the desperate woman and carrying her to the couch in the other room.

10

The next morning Marosi called Major Blindics, whom Livia Kismányoki had mentioned in the hospital. After a few probing questions, the receptionist told him that Blindics worked in the homicide division, and that his first name was László. Blindics turned out to be very obliging, once Marosi had introduced himself by name and military rank, and had explained that he called because of Eva Szalánczky, who had been shot at the border by his people. They arranged a meeting for the next day at the police station.

Marosi got dressed, ate his breakfast alone and took off for a stroll in the city.

The first stop was the hospital. He didn't want to admit it to himself, but his curiosity was no longer limited to Eva Szalánczky. "Many sins can only be committed by someone who has many reasons to sin." Only a great personality can inspire so many sins. This woman must be someone special, if she could provoke her husband to attempt murder.

It seemed as if Livia had been waiting for him. With wide open eyes, she motioned him to pull a chair closer to her. Even closer. When Marosi sat down, she asked in a whisper: "Was it suicide?"

Marosi stopped short. "Why should it have been suicide?"

"Because she had tried it once before . . . What happened this time?"

"She tried to cross the border illegally, and she was shot."

"My god! My god!" Horrified, Livia closed her eyes. "Why did she want to leave? She and this country were of one piece. She could try to cut herself loose, but she would die in the process . . . How could she not know this? How could she not take this into consideration? She saw everything so terribly clearly—including herself . . . Half a year ago she said—"

Marosi leaned closer. "What?"

"'If I go on like this, sooner or later someone will kill me.'"

They fell silent. The first lieutenant saw the shaken face, and he asked very softly: "Why did your husband want to kill you?"

Livia declined: "That's a long story."

She looked around without lifting her head from the pillow. The old woman in the bed next to her was asleep, and all the other patients were busy with something. They had gotten used to the idea that occasionally Mrs. Horváth was interrogated by plainclothes police. But it did not prevent them from asking the resident doctor why this troublemaking patient wasn't moved to a special room. The overcrowded hospital, where at times patients had to be put in the hallways, did not have the space for that.

"Since I'm here in the hospital, I have lots of time to reflect," Livia said and looked at Marosi. "I've ordered a bunch of books, but I simply can't get myself to read . . . 'The fog that has engulfed my life has now receded/How far from the hills of death my glance wanders.'

"Today I know that everything was wrong right from the beginning . . . Five years ago, I received my teacher's credential. I was sent to a village to work. I was in an elementary school which only employed two teachers. I was teaching the older children, the higher grades; the younger ones were supervised by a twenty-year-old. He had a soft, almost feminine face, a gigantic Adam's apple, and he always wore dazzling white shirts. Of course, we didn't have a teacher's room, we always talked in the classroom which smelled of the oils used to treat the floor. I sat at the teacher's desk and he on top of one of the school benches.

"'Is there a library in the village?' I asked him once.

"'Yes . . . yes. There is a book case in town hall.'

"'You don't get books to read from there?'

"'I haven't read anything in two years.'

"'You don't have time for it?'

"'I've got plenty of time. I just don't have any desire.'

"'How about newspapers, magazines?'

"'I can't even keep up with all the bureaucratic communiques. You'll find out one day.'

"'There is a cultural center, I know, because I live in one of the cloakrooms. But is it ever used?'

"'Three dances took place there during the winter.'

"'Isn't there a youth organization in this village?'

"'Yes.'

"'Who is the secretary?'

"'I.'

"'What do you do with the young people?'

"'Nothing. The year before last, when I arrived here, I got busy. We put on a few plays, a few folk dances. After that, the young people didn't show up anymore.'

"'Why not?'

"'Because I started to flirt with one of the young girls.'

"'Only because of that?'

"At first his answers had been indifferent, almost resigned. But now a mocking, pained smile was on his face. and for the first time there was a bit of life in him.

"'You don't know this village yet.'

"'And what about the theater?'

"'That's in the city. Forty forints for the ride, twenty for the ticket, forty for the hotel. It's not worth all that.'

"The young man had something slimy, something dis-

71

agreeable about him, that's why I was angry with him and not the situation—nevertheless I felt a certain horror.

"When we walked home from school, he asked me: 'Which side of the road do you live on?'

"'In the cultural center,' I repeated.

"'The other side then.' He looked at my high-heeled shoes. 'Do you have rubber boots?'

"'No.'

"'Buy a pair. Or move to this side of the road. When it rains, it's impossible to walk through the mud without rubber boots.'

"Five people in the village had a certain standing. The postmistress, the veterinarian, the agricultural expert and we two teachers. I thought that we should get together and do something for the village's cultural life. The postmistress was an honest, simple widow with three school-age children. She could barely breathe because she had to cook, wash, clean and watch her children all the time . . . I told her about the Hungarian Women's Association, and how useful it would be to get organized.

"'I have nothing against it, comrade,' she said. 'I've gone to all the meetings to which I was invited. I know to whom I owe my position.' But she wasn't willing to comprehend anything beyond that.

"The veterinarian and the agronomist worked themselves to the bone. Culture for them was confined to the question of whether they should get drunk on beer or on cognac after work.

"There were many reasonable people in the village. Still, there was nothing I could do. Not even as much as my predecessor, the teacher with the pretty face. He had failed, because he had begun a simple flirtation. A handsome twenty-year-old teacher is a good match, at least a better one than an average farmer, who has to pay too many taxes. At the beginning, every mother of a daughter could fantasize him as her future son-in-law and sent her daughter to the youth organization in order to be shown off. When the teacher showed interest in one, overnight he was no longer attractive for the others. When, on top of it, he didn't marry the girl, the village excluded him more and more, as if he had the plague. In this village, the medieval moral code still prevailed: a young man was considered a groom if he danced with the same girl twice.

"I was also marked because of my beauty. The women were jealous, they hated me and they kept their men from me. The men, though—including the senile librarian, the secretary of the youth organization (he was sixteen and I had picked him rather than my colleague), the council's secretary (a graduate of the Red Academy)—misinterpreted, some sooner, others later, my educational attempts. They would rather have seen me on my back, especially since I wasn't interested. They spread rumors, that I had an affair with the chair of the co-operative, with my colleague and with the pub owner. Each of the three knew that it wasn't true, but each believed it of the others and obviously they thought, 'if the others are successful, why not me?'

"I wasn't interested in supplying the village with daily gossip, and I retreated from my social activities. But without them, living in the village was unbearable. I liked being in school, teaching was good for me, and I had three exceptional and two smart children. An actor or lecturer who discovers only one eager pair of eyes in the audience will try to engage the indifferent ones, even if it takes hypnosis. There were five eager pairs of eyes waiting for me every day. Unfortunately, I'm not very talented," her face had darkened, "but . . ."

"Not talented in writing?" Marosi interrupted her discreetly.

"No."

*What made her turn to journalism? What made her think she
could be an editor?* Marosi thought.

". . . but I have a good sense for the arts. Music, dance,
drawing, poetry, that's where I was able to contribute something. At school, I felt like an infatuated woman making
love. I gathered the children in various working groups
. . . but still I had lots of time on my hands. Those terrible
long winter evenings! It's impossible to read forever. Sometimes I was overcome by such a ghastly feeling, I forgot to
talk. I was afraid that I would end up like my handsome
colleague. Then I counted the stitches in my crochet work,
and I had no time to think of anything else.

"One day, I received the final blow. Kovács, the district's
inspector of schools, came to see us. A forty-year-old,
coarse, morose man, who (so I was told) was an air force
officer during the war. This is not a judgment. I'm just
mentioning it as part of the biography. He attended all the
lessons, and afterwards pompously passed *his* judgment
and invited us to the pub. My colleague agreed without
any comment, and I did the same, thinking that he was
used to local customs. Out of politeness, I drank a glass of
wine before saying farewell. The inspector asked me to
stay, but I pressed upon him that I had papers to grade.

"It was a clear winter day, and I wanted to go for a walk.
In the village, it would have been impossible, because the
women would have thought that the Budapest whore was
walking the streets. I walked a good distance from the
village on a path through a frozen field, and returned only
when it got dark. On the other side of the road, I saw a
man and when I got closer, I saw that it was Kovács. He
must have recognized me too, because he stopped. I had
no desire to talk to him. I looked away and continued to
walk. I noticed that he turned around and followed me on
the opposite side of the road. I didn't know this person,
but after my experience in the morning, I had a bad impres-

sion of him. I got scared and I started to walk faster. Without turning around, I opened the front door of the cultural center and slammed it behind me.

"I was still behind the door when he arrived. I didn't turn on the light; I thought maybe it would be possible to mislead him. In the dark, I went to the cloakroom, where I was staying. Nobody was living in the cultural center, not even the administrator. Kovács hammered on the front door. I locked the cloakroom and listened. My whole body was trembling with fear. He only needed to kick in the glass of the front door—the door of the cloakroom consisted of a very thin particle board with a ridiculous lock. If this heavy man with his broad shoulders leaned against it, it would break open. In the twentieth century, I would be raped in the middle of a village. And on top of it: who would believe me? Insistently, he hammered against the front door, while I stood in the dark and waited for the clinking of shattering glass.

"One hour passed, maybe more. I could not count on the villagers. Desperation gave me courage. I took the flashlight (which one always needed to go out at night) and in the dark, I slipped softly to the front door and suddenly aimed the flashlight through the glass and straight into his face. I thought this would startle him into returning to his lodgings. He was drunk; he twisted his face and grinned broadly and stupidly. I blinded him for at least five minutes, and then I turned off the flashlight and returned to my room. Now I dared to turn on the light. I picked up a half-meter-long poker, and I tried to gauge how much force I would need to hit him with it. I was calm. With this heavy iron, it would be possible to crack someone's head open; and believe me, I would have done it. At that moment, I thought I was strong enough to kill the school inspector. After an hour, he got sick of knocking on that door and it became quiet. I put the poker at the head of my bed and went to sleep.

"The next morning, I saw him on my way to school. He was waiting at the bus stop. He greeted me coldly. I returned his greetings, but I felt a shiver running down my spine. I realized that if this person was not master of my life and my death, he was at least my employer.

"I wanted to finish the school year honorably, and then ask for a transfer. Not necessarily to Budapest, but somewhere in an industrial region. I understand the language of workers better. My father is a worker, a leather cutter in a shoe factory.

"But the inspector would have never agreed to a transfer, this I could read clearly in his face. The only option left was to rot in this village, or to start another profession.

"A few weeks later a former admirer from my Budapest years appeared in a brand-new first lieutenant's uniform. He said that he had gotten an official residence, and that I should become his wife . . ."

"Your husband is a soldier?" Marosi asked, surprised.

"A teaching officer," the young woman said. Her face appeared tired, she wanted to end the conversation. She asked Marosi to give her some lemonade from her bedside table. Softly, he put his left arm under her neck, lifted her head a bit and put the glass in her hand, touching her hot skin. A comforting stir went through his body.

"Thanks," Livia said. "My husband taught military science at my college. That's how we met. In short, he asked for my hand. 'You don't have to give me an answer right away,' he said when he saw my hesitation. 'Tomorrow morning before I leave, I'll ask you again.'

"The next morning a pair of rubber boots made the decision for me. I hated those boots because of their smell. I agreed to his proposal and together we went to Budapest."

Livia closed her eyes. Marosi looked at her, without excitement, but with a painful pleasure as if he was looking at a masterfully crafted statue.

76

How beautiful she is, he thought. *Why didn't she find a better husband?* He remembered that in Eva Szalánczky's notes he had read: *a small, inert officer.*

"Go," Livia asked without opening her eyes.

"I've only got one more question," Marosi requested apologetically. "Did you love him?"

"In those days, yes. But . . . I was mostly thankful."

Marosi got up. He pressed the small, well-formed hand which rested ineffectually on the bed cover. She kept her eyes closed.

"May I come back tomorrow?"

"Sure, come." She looked at him for a second. Her eyes were green, like the eyes of a cat.

A woman who left her fate to a pair of rubber boots.

11

M arosi went back to the editor's office. Erdös' secretary, an attractive, dark-haired woman who was slightly older than the lieutenant, greeted him like an old acquaintance. She smiled regretfully:

"Comrade Editor-in-Chief is dictating the lead story."

"I didn't want to see him," Marosi said. "Tell me, does one of your employees have a thin mustache?"

"Yes. Attila Hagymási. Down the hall to your left, the third door."

Marosi found a tall, clean-shaven man sitting hunched over one of the two desks. He was telling someone on the phone that he would be at the horse races on Sunday. He motioned his visitor to take a seat. *That's not Attila Hagymási,* Marosi thought and remained standing.

"What can I do for you?" the man asked and hung up the phone.

"I wanted to speak with Attila Hagymási . . ."

"He's in the province on a story. He'll be back on Monday." When Marosi didn't move, he asked: "Can I give him a message?"

Marosi hesitated. "I wanted to talk to him about Eva Szalánczky."

The man became serious: "Poor Eva . . . I'm really sorry . . . When I think of her, I hear Fortinbras saying that if she had lived long enough, she could have been a great queen."

"Did you know Eva?"

"I? . . . Better than Attila."

78

Marosi introduced himself. With no small amount of charm, he explained in detail why he was interested in Eva Szalánczky's fate.

"There is a little pub downstairs," the journalist said and tidied his desk. "Let's go. By the way, I'm Zoltán Fiala." Once in the pub, they sat down at one of the tables in the corner and ordered red wine. Greedily, Fiala drank two glasses. He propped his elbows up on the table, his fists kneading his cheeks.

"I loved Eva very dearly. I especially admired her talent, her strength, her unwillingness to compromise . . . Interestingly, she used to say that she lacked the ability to compromise. That wasn't a virtue, just a fact." Fiala looked at Marosi. "For many years, I came to the office without pleasure. Only my body was here; I left my eyes and ears—my soul—at home. I didn't know anything about anyone. I wasn't interested. Each week, I wrote what was required of me, and then I pursued my own life. The clever and courageous remarks Eva Szalánczky made during editorial meetings caught my attention, but not enough to try to get to know her . . . It was very difficult to get close to Eva; she was an inaccessible, tough person . . . But once . . ."

Zoltán Fiala wasn't heavy, but he had a fleshy face, which, despite some scrubby whiskers, lacked any masculinity whatsoever. Nevertheless, the rather feminine face was appealing due to its delicate melancholy. Memories of Eva made his face sharper, livelier and more expressive. He drank his wine in one gulp.

"Once—it was last February—the old guy ordered us to go to Szolnok county. They were in the process of establishing a producers' co-operative. It was already in the hundredth or so village. We were told to check it out, see how it was done and if it was a good thing. In the early morning, we left Budapest in one car: Livia, Eva and I. Jani was our driver. I like to start the day with brandy, and I had a small flask in my pocket. It was gone by the time we reached

Szolnok. We got our hotel rooms, ate breakfast and went to meet the Party committee. We received our instructions there. Each of us was assigned to a county official who was responsible for collectivization in a different village.

"In the evening, we met in the hotel. We invited the officials to dinner, and together we discussed our experiences. At the beginning, our talk focused exclusively on the producers' co-operative." He looked at Marosi. "If you are interested in Eva Szalánczky's opinion on the subject, I can tell you all about it, because we discussed our impressions of the visit a few days later at the newspaper office But first, I would like to talk about something else, which I consider more important . . .

"After dinner, we started drinking . . . You mentioned that you talked to Livia in the hospital. Well . . . What can I say? . . . She isn't who she used to be. The shooting changed her completely. The most striking thing about her was not that she was a beautiful woman who knew how to show it, but that she was very sexual. Sensuality flowed out of every pore. Her vanity was boundless. Coquetry and the craving for conquest were deeply embedded in her, and so instinctive that you could say those were the strongest components of her personality. She couldn't stand it if people were indifferent towards her, not only men, but also children, women, old people, every helper, every driver.

"Well, we were sitting in that restaurant, drinking. Two women and four men. The atmosphere became more and more relaxed. We dropped the 'comrade' and we drank with them and pledged friendship, told little anecdotes and reactionary jokes. Livia was flirting with everyone . . . slowly, each of her words had a double meaning. You know how these things develop . . . And, really, there were not two women present, just one, because Livia was the absolute center. One of the officials, a huge coarse man, snorted and grunted, his scabby mouth dribbled, his paunch welled out over his pants, and he had forgotten to close his fly. He was sweating, and his shirt was greasy. For Livia, only one thing counted—to conquer even this uninviting peddler. Of course, she succeeded. The further the evening progressed, the less Eva participated in the performance. Finally, she got up and said gravely: 'Excuse me!' and left us. She looked disgusted with Livia."

Fiala ordered another half liter of wine. "When do you usually eat?" he asked Marosi.

"It doesn't matter. I have a soldier's stomach."

"Then let's eat later . . . After Eva had left for her room," Fiala continued with his story, "it seemed as if a thousand watt lamp had gone out in Livia. She became passive, absent-minded, yes, even cross. I couldn't get rid of the notion that she was playing a role for Eva, that she wanted to be the star of Eva's stage. She no longer responded to the siege of the lecherous men and shortly afterwards dismissed everyone. We separated. I have to confess that I was disappointed—that little beast had aroused me quite a bit." Thoughtfully, he drank some wine.

"It wasn't until the next morning that I realized that we had been given three adjoining rooms, otherwise I would have gone into Livia's room . . . I got undressed and quickly fell asleep. I don't know how long I had been sleeping when I was startled out of my sleep by a sweetly smelling naked body crawling into bed with me. It was Livia. 'I'm afraid to be alone,' she whispered. I didn't understand why a person would be afraid to be alone in a hotel, but as you can imagine, I was pleased . . . At the hospital you couldn't see the gorgeous body of this woman. She is tall, slender, but not skinny, she has well proportioned, full thighs, firm breasts and is pure passion . . . Excuse me, my friend, because I get lost in such details, but it is important for what follows. I wasn't in good shape because of all that drinking and I would have fallen asleep after the first time, but she kept touching me, until . . . She stayed with me until dawn, but I couldn't really satisfy her . . . She kissed me good-bye, I heard her go into her room, turn off the light. I heard how her bed creaked.

"All of a sudden, the door of my room was opened gently. Hushed steps came closer, someone stood at the head of my bed, knife in hand, ready to plunge it into my throat. Mistakenly, I thought I recognized Eva Szalánczky. Strangely enough, I wasn't surprised, as if I had always known that this woman, whom I hardly knew, was passionate enough to murder. I didn't dare move. Totally frozen, I waited for the thrust as fair punishment. I pulled myself together. Drenched with sweat, I turned on the light. Of course, there was nobody in the room."

Little by little, the hall filled with people, and the waiters rattled trays of dishes.

"Let's order some food," Fiala suggested, "otherwise we'll be asked to leave. I can go on talking while we eat."

The selection was poor. They could choose from only three meat dishes, Wiener Schnitzel, veal cutlet and pork stew. They ordered pork stew and pickles. Fiala continued with his story:

"The next day on our way back, everybody was sleepy, hungover, spiritless. Livia was sitting in front next to the driver, and she didn't say a word during the whole trip. Maybe she was ashamed, I don't know. I was dozing, and Eva was taking notes or writing a poem. I didn't look. It was already dark by the time we arrived in Budapest. First, we took Livia home. Her good-bye was cold; she didn't even shake hands with us. Then, I took Eva to Buda. She didn't get out. 'I would like to talk to you,' she said. 'Let's go somewhere if you've got time.' She seemed ominous, dramatic. I remembered my dream of the knife. We asked the driver to take us to an espresso and then sent him home. I ordered cognac. Eva drank hers immediately, and then she looked into my eyes and nailed me with her question: 'Livia spent the night with you?'"

Fiala looked at Marosi. "My dear fellow, I've lent my handkerchief to many women to dry more tears than I can count. I thought that Eva wanted to complain, about life, the newspaper, the government. Sometimes women need to pour out their hearts. Most often, they start by saying: 'My mother never liked me.' But her question came as such a surprise to me, confused me, and, at that moment, I couldn't think of a lie. I admitted it.

"'She promised to spend the night with me,' she said bitterly. 'That was the only reason why I came along. Originally, I had arranged with the old guy to do the report on my own . . . She really took me in . . .' You know, my friend," Fiala continued, "I like courageous people . . ."

He fell silent because the waiter showed up with the pork stew. They ate heartily. As bachelors, they knew that they would never be cheated with two restaurant entrees: kettle goulash and meat stew. Everything else required expertise, a feeling for cooking and attention. All of which were hardly considerations in the restaurant business during those meager years. Meat stew only needed onions, paprika and meat.

"So," Fiala went on with his story between two bites, "I like courageous people. Probably because I'm not. Erasmus wrote: 'They say I'm not courageous. That would make me very sad if I were the leader of the uhlans. But I'm only a poor poet' . . . Eva Szalánczky didn't know about jealousy, deviousness, or even how to talk around a topic. Either she was silent—she *really* knew how to be silent—or she didn't mince words." Fiala was done with his meal; he finished his glass of wine, wiped his mouth and lit a cigarette. "Eva and I talked intimately until closing time, as if we had known each other since childhood. There was no barrier between us, no constraint. Concepts such as freedom, responsibility, success, money, family, love, death meant the same to both of us. In Eva, I saw myself when I was young and had just set out on my own."

He was silent and, with a bitter smile, stared at the wine-stained tablecloth.

"You know," he confessed haltingly, "my generation went through so much, it is almost a miracle that we are not more rotten than we actually are. I gave up believing in anything a long time ago, least of all the written word. We have lied so much . . ." Slightly tipsy, he looked at Marosi. "Why didn't I just say to hell with journalism? Because I didn't know anything else and I'm too old to re-train as a sheet metal worker or nurse . . . or a useful human being."

Absent-mindedly, he poured more wine in their glasses.

"While I was talking with Eva, I was taken, completely intoxicated, and I had the illusion that I could be just like her . . . that she could change me, and that I could change her with the power of male passion . . . I took her home and wanted to come up to her room.

"'My room is cold,' she said apologetically, 'and I don't have the energy to get a fire started.'

"'I'll do it.'

"'Another time, Zoltán,' she put me off gently.

"'I love you,' I said and kissed her in the doorway.

"'I love you, too.' She did not withdraw her mouth from mine."

Fiala was silent. Partially, because the memory was painful, but also because the waiter was clearing the dirty dishes. Only the bread crumbs were left, which Fiala swept from the table with the side of his hand.

"The next day, I slept at her house. In a shabby sublet room, which I would not have traded for a mansion in Hawaii. I think we both were happy . . ."

His mouth was twisted in a solemn smile . . .

"In some respect, men are always insecure. That's why I asked her afterwards: 'Was it nice, my dear?' We talked a lot . . . But it was never enough. I mentioned before that I was working at the newspaper 'without eyes and ears', and that I knew nothing about anything. Eva told me that Livia was the editor-in-chief's lover. They had worked together in the archive. The old guy brought her along when he was offered the position at the newspaper. But Eva also told me that Livia liked neither her husband nor her lover, and that most probably she was frigid. That's why she was screwing every Tom, Dick and Harry—in order to find someone who could show her what love was all about. Eva also told me that Livia was an untalented journalist, but she compensated for it by trying to conquer everybody, not only every man, but also every woman."

Fiala lifted his head. "Strangely enough, we almost always talked about Livia during those intimate moments."

He poured more wine in his glass. "She told me how everything had started between them. It was Eva's third day at work at the newspaper. She had an admirer whom she couldn't stand, and every morning he waited in front of her house for her. He escorted her to the tramway stop, because he wanted to see her at least for those few minutes in order to make his day friendlier or more bearable. On the morning in question, he had brought her a bunch of lilies of the valley. It was the beginning of spring. Eva took the flowers to the paper, where she shared an office with Livia. Since she didn't know her way around, she asked Livia where she could find a vase. Livia jumped up and said she would get one. She arranged the flowers in the vase and disappeared from the room. As you know, unlike Livia, Eva had worked for a newspaper before 1956, and she had a number of professional friends and colleagues. By accident, she met one of her colleagues that evening and roaring with laughter, he told her: 'Imagine Livia Kismányoki came storming into our office today and gave us the latest hot gossip. Eva Szalánczky had already started to lay a trap for her by bringing her lilies of the valley.' Eva got really angry. The next morning she said to Livia in the editorial meeting room: 'You are wrong Livia, if you think that I'm attracted to you. With your body, I would get claustrophobic even in a stand-up pub.' Livia turned scarlet and left the room in a hurry. But it seemed as if she had made up her mind and wanted to prove that even Eva Szalánczky would not get claustrophobic with a body like hers around. Systematically, she started to seduce Eva, driving her crazy. The end of the story was that Eva fell in love with her."

Fiala's eyes were blurred. He poured more wine.

"My marriage is totally rotten. Our children are grown up. Who the hell knows where they are. My wife picked up a twenty-five-year-old soccer player who can do it all night. I can't do that. I'm old. I asked Eva to live with me; maybe we could help each other. She thought about it for a week and then she said 'no.' Our farewell talk lasted a long time. 'I can't change any more,' she said, discouraged. 'Maybe I don't want to change. My "disease" is as old as humanity. Sin is much more recent. Sin is only a diabolical invention of society. But calling it an illness, and not a sin, which is how most of society considers it—I know that very well—allows me to at least see myself as a tragic heroine and not as a weak-minded, incompetent, pitiable plague-blister. Tell me, Zoltán, why am I neither perfectly normal nor perfectly abnormal?'"

Fiala called the waiter, rejecting Marosi's offer to pay: "I invited *you*. You did me a favor by letting me talk about Eva Szalánczky. It was painful—I wish I could have saved her. And still, you didn't make me feel I had been humiliated. I love the lines by Attila József: 'Blessed—because I'm living forever—the one who buried me for one night . . .' I buried her several nights, believing that I might make her life a bit easier . . . but I was not successful."

86

12

A mong Eva's notes, Marosi had found a few pages which hadn't made any sense to him. Now he re-read them.

"As if you had heard it from a church choir: You were beautiful, Livia, my noble one, my light; you were like a fir tree, sweetly smelling, you were like powdery snow, like a snow-covered mountain top; you were like a holiday. Mirrors changed colors, reflected you in all devotion, and you became intoxicated with the power of your beauty. I became more and more upset every time I looked at you, but you were not able to see the fire in my eyes.

"I jumped up. 'Excuse me,' I said and ran out of the room. The lights had died out, and instead of the mirror's devoted reflection, there was the smell of cheap liquor and cigarette smoke. You'd lost your audience, because the one you were playing for had left. And you realized how meager the setting had been, the men drunk and vulgar.

"You lay down in this wretched hotel room, the door locked behind you. You wanted to lock me out, in order to preserve the illusion of choice.

"I was in the next room, separated from you by only the thin wall. I heard you throw off your shoes, brush your teeth; I heard your bed's rusty springs receive your body.

"You were waiting for a knock.

"You smoked two cigarettes, but no one knocked. Then you sneaked to the door barefoot, and you turned the key without making a sound. And, again, you lit a cigarette, but you couldn't smoke it to the end, because it tasted bitter, like bile.

"Bitter, like my face, when I left you there on the vain and cheap stage of your games.

"All of a sudden, you were hit by the thought that I would not come to you. Of course I wouldn't—you would have only played with me, since that's how you behaved with everyone.

"You opened the door of your room a bit, looked up and down the hall. A row of doors hid their secrets in the flickering light. Yours in the middle, mine to the left, and the man's to the right. From his room escaped soft snoring; from mine, silence. Then you knew that I was still awake, stretched out on the bed in my clothes, waiting, with the same bitter expression on my face with which I had left the restaurant.

"You closed the door, and it was as if you had exhaled all the air from the room. You were overcome by bodily discomfort; you felt like you were suffocating. You felt that you couldn't stand it for very long, at best an hour or two. You became afraid. Of the walls, of the silence, of yourself. You threw your beautiful, idle body on the bed, and it seemed as if it got caught in barbed wire. Then you walked back and forth from one piece of hostile furniture to the next, pressed your face against the window, stared out into the night of a strange city. The night is never as indifferent as during the winter.

"Why is no window opening into the chaos of your soul?

"Why am I not with you to help you?

"A human being *is* her life, but the life of a human being is not always adequate for her. What did I say last night, when we decided to go to the province together? Most of us go with the flow—a skill we learn from society and the families we are born into—because we fail to examine society's mechanisms. If we do, we get scared and turn away from the abyss opening up in front of us. But, if the human being wants to become truly herself, if she wants to be a real person, with an individual and indispensable face, then she must not turn away from herself. She has to take her life into her own hands, the same way a sculptor takes material in hand, giving shape to an idea that emerged formlessly from his soul. This requires an incredible amount of courage. It's a path leading through crisis, doubt and uncertainties.

"Do you know what came to my mind when I turned eighteen and thus came of age? Not that I was now eligible to vote, that I could get married without my parents' permission, or that I could receive an inheritance—should there be one—but that from this day on I could be hanged for a crime which yesterday would have just sent me to a reformatory. In other words, I was thinking about the law . . . Every human being is immortal, because we live on in our children, in our friends, and in people we don't know, whom we have only influenced in the slightest way—but not everyone deserves well of humanity. I decided that I wouldn't do anything for which I could be hanged, but I also would not neglect anything which would make eternity worth the effort . . . 'The conformist merely takes up space provided in a world which could do just as well without him.'

"Once, when you were a teacher in a small village, you longed for more. You also didn't accept life as a given. You also wanted change . . .

"Each of my words passed through your mind, and each of my words led you to me, like a funnel drawing fluid.

"You put on your robe, left the room, and directed your hesitating steps towards my door. You felt like a stone, which thrown away can only obey one law, the law of gravity, the endurance of free fall. You felt this fall once before in your life, as ecstasy; in the hallway, you remembered it was when you gave birth.

"Why did you have a child with him, if you don't love him? Did you want to tie him down anyway? Did you need to prove yourself?

"No! No! If this had been the case, you would have admitted it. You simply wanted to have a child. You wanted to bring a child into this world because you were young, beautiful and healthy. You wanted to give another human being the possibility of enjoying life. A life which, in the end, is all hers. You didn't bring this child into the world for your husband, you birthed her for yourself. You wanted to have a reason to live—knowing that this human being would always mean a lot for you; but also knowing that one day she'd leave you. You knew that this would be painful; nevertheless, you went ahead—this was the most noble aspect of this experience.

"Your daughter is now three, and the separation process has already started. You have already perceived that being a mother causes more pain, more sorrow than joy . . . This living blood circulation of emotions is majestic . . . is a constant succession of waves, an open sea, an endless perspective opening one new door after the other. Not the source of happiness, but more. As you were stumbling towards a new beginning in the hotel hallway, you knew: what you have learned in life so far is not the best, but something else whose name you couldn't know.

"You live in an iron cast, which others have molded for you. It's true, the mold slipped a bit and left you full of complexes, pangs of consciousness and searching. But you are not without protection, because the old iron form is still sticking to you. Drastic world events do not reach your open nerves, but only this armor, and therefore they hurt less. This mold, which was created by others, naturally can only be destroyed if you also destroy some parts of yourself.

"But what will happen if you don't have the strength to rebuild yourself out of the fragments?

"You knew that this night held no existential question for me. There is only one human being without whom I can't live: that's me. Maybe you would have come to my room if I hadn't confessed that, but if I had lied like the others: 'I can't live without you.' Humans love to think that others can't live without them. We make ourselves believe that the universe can't be without us. But I don't lie, and I can't stand other people's lies.

"You don't know how you reached the man's room. His glance bore more astonishment than joy.

"You threw your robe on the floor, you lay down right next to him. The nightgown—as usual—was taken off by the man. Everything happened in the customary way and he didn't see your lies."

Did the rubber boots decide again, Marosi mused, *or not this time?*

13

M arosi arrived at the branch of the Ervin Szabó Library just before closing. He asked for Magda Módra. The cloakroom attendant sent him to a first floor office whose door was marked "Library Director." He knocked and entered. The only window in the room faced a dirty fire wall ridden with bullet holes. The room did not have enough light.

A small woman sat in the light of a desk lamp—pale skin, pale hair, the sharp nose stuck out of her thin face. She looked at Marosi not only with suspicion, but also with fear. Marosi, who was not in uniform, introduced himself and explained in detail why he had come. Magda Módra buried her face in her hands. Small, bony hands.

"I've already heard that she is dead. Horrible!" she said after a while, and got up and took off her blue work smock. "Working hours are almost over, let's go somewhere."

Magda Módra was small, skinny, flat as an ironing board and looked as if she was thirteen-years-old. Only her head was big, and her face was lined with sharp wrinkles. Marosi tried to imagine her downy loins. He was disgusted.

She must have been twenty-five or twenty-six. Her movements were hesitant, awkward, insecure. *She has as much energy,* Marosi thought, *as a broken chair that's been thrown on a garbage pile and is now expected to blossom into flower.*

They went to a nearby outdoor café. There was some street noise, and the early September dusk brought a refreshing breeze.

"What do you want? Cognac? Coffee?" Marosi asked.

"Both to start out," Magda Módra said with an embarrassed smile. "Eva and I always started like that . . . Later, we just stuck to cognac."

"Did Eva drink?" Marosi asked.

"Of course . . . Who doesn't? Everybody drinks. Only those whose livers can no longer bear it, stop."

Magda Módra smiled intimately at the slightly older waitress whose features were rather masculine.

"I greet you, Magda. What would you like to have?"

"The waitress knows you?" Marosi asked, after he had ordered.

"I've come here for eight years," Magda explained. "As long as I had no flat, I studied and read here. My love life was celebrated here. This is where I was sad and where I used to write my poetry."

"You write poetry?" Marosi was surprised.

"I'm a poet," said the small woman, whose body had stopped growing.

Marosi complimented her, but at the same time, he thought: *It's easier to believe that she writes poems than that she has a love life.*

The drinks came, and they clinked glasses. While Marosi was still putting his glass to his mouth, Magda had already finished her drink.

Alcoholic, Marosi thought. *She won't get up from a table as long as there is a bottle of brandy on top.* "Would you like to have another one?" he asked.

"A little bit later," the woman answered. "Once, I didn't find Eva at the newspaper and I went to her flat. She laid there with a wet cloth on her head. I had to think of a poem: 'Either she'll die right now, or we'll see a miracle!'" She laughed happily. "Eva didn't dare get up, she was too weak. She had been throwing up all day long. She sent me out to get her beer, ham and biscuits. I helped her get well again. After only an hour, she wanted . . ." Magda Módra fell silent.

"How long have you known Eva?"

"Since university. We were in the same year . . . But we only got to know each other better when I was released from jail . . ." She interrupted herself and gave the man a scared look.

Marosi called the waitress. He was surprised because she did not show up to take his order, but arrived with two cognacs. Magda drank her second one as greedily as the first. *I have to get her drunk,* Marosi thought.

"Did you spend time in jail because of 1956?" he asked.

"Because of my poems," the woman said with an undertone of false modesty.

"After 1956 then?"

"Yes."

"For how long?"

"One year. Together with detention awaiting trial, eighteen months."

"Where have your poems been published?"

"That's the reason. In an illegal newspaper."

"Don't you want to recite one of your poems for me?"

"No. Even today this would be considered agitation."

"I wasn't necessarily thinking of a political poem," Marosi said with a charming smile. "You know I'm a hardened soldier. The last thing I read was *Puszta in the Winter* . . . Don't hold it against me if I don't know your poetry.

The small, ugly woman underwent an astonishing transformation. The pale skin on her face flushed, the sharp lines softened, and her look became dreamy. *Just like a woman during lovemaking,* Marosi thought. Her lips shivered as she began to recite her poem:

Doris, to me you will always be Dorothy—
What makes you cry, washing dishes at home?

94

If you were unloved
Where would you find solace?
What would you—lacking a better word—call home-
     sickness?

It was not I who created the barriers,
or made my heart a no man's land, a waste land.
This piece of flesh that even yesterday was wide open,
waiting
for someone who would not have humiliated me.

Once, I wore opportunity like a big nose or a big heart,
I was shapeless like flames.
Was I a prodigy, or was I just garbage?
Now, when hope dies, nobody knows what dies
          with it,
and my grave stone will be the last—because those who
forget me
will also be made of stone."

After she finished, she was silent and stared at the table.
Preoccupied, she twisted her cognac glass in her small,
bony hand. Softly, Marosi touched the back of her hand,
searched for her look.

"Very beautiful," he said warmly.

The woman winced.

"Let's drink," she said desperately, and signaled the waitress with two fingers. "You know, when I got out of jail, I
found out that my girlfriend had left the country. My family
disowned me. As long as I was imprisoned, I received visits
from my mother and my sister. They sent packages, when
it was permitted, because they didn't want to abandon me
to 'disgrace and shame.' But as soon as I was released,
they showed me the door, because I had brought shame
to the family, and they no longer wanted to know me. In

vain, I explained to them that I hadn't done anything, except write a few poems, which reflected neither the official ideology nor its opposite. I tried to imagine a third way: a Hungarian way."

She kept silent as long as the waitress was cleaning off the table. Then she continued: "My sister is the wife of a high Party functionary. My family disowned me to prevent my compromising the two." She drank her cognac. "You know in that ill-fated trial of the woman doctor, I was also one of the accused, even though . . . my name appeared in the papers a few times . . . even though there were *two* resistance groups, who had nothing in common. But, autocratically, the judge linked them together based on the fact that the two groups had been stationed in the same hospital, and we found out about each other one or two days before the defeat . . . The doctor and her followers were armed resistance fighters, they patrolled the district around the Eastern Railway Station, and they fired on Russian tanks and patrols. They killed a young man who had joined them, because they believed that he was an informer. The doctor gave him a water injection . . ."

"That was after November fourth, wasn't it?"

"Yes. Until November fourth, we were working on our newspaper in the publishing house. When the Russians started to fire at the city at dawn on the fourth, we went into hiding in the cellar of the hospital where the doctor was working. She had killed that young man there in her office . . . Shall we order another one?"

Marosi waved, and within seconds the drinks were in front of them. Magda Módra continued with her story:

"There in the cellar, besides writing poetry, I was ordered—knowing nothing about the murder which had taken place on the first floor—to listen to Radio Free Europe. I had to type out the interesting news and put it in the paper. Also my poems . . ."

She drank the cognac. In the meantime, it had gotten dark, and the garden was filled with people coming off work.

"The court believed me when I testified that I had nothing to do with the murder. That's why I got only one year. But my own sister, my own mother didn't believe me . . . I got out of jail and I had no flat, and I couldn't find work in my field. My girlfriend had defected. I started work in a textile factory and that's how I ended up on a cot in one of the workers' lodgings. The poem is from that time period."

They nursed their silence, hopelessly, for a long time. Marosi ordered another round of cognacs. Softly, he pushed her:

"What about Eva Szalánczky?"

Magda Módra was on the verge of being drunk. She was suspended in that place where one is liberated from one's inhibitions, but still clinging to the chains of reason.

"They sent two detectives after me, to try to recruit me as an informer . . . You know," she looked befuddled at Marosi, ". . . those who have left jail are always surrounded with nets . . . They do whatever they can . . . The two were constantly on my heels. If I sat down in an espresso, they sat down at the same table. When I went to the movies, they bought the tickets to the seats right next to mine. They waited for me at the factory gate, they followed me home, they whispered in my ear, they promised work in my field."

"As a librarian?" Marosi asked.

"Yes. They promised me a scholarship and a flat . . . When all that failed, they tried to blackmail me. In vain, I tried to get protection from my former teachers, my colleagues. The two detectives made sure that I never got anywhere. Not only because of my political past, but . . ."

She looked directly at Marosi and watched his reaction: "I'm a lesbian."

Marosi's face remained motionless. Magda Módra was

relieved. "Well, today that is no longer one of the crimes for which one gets imprisoned. But it's enough to provoke contempt . . . And they tried to convince me that not only turncoats were approached to provide this service. Metternich's informers, for example, were famous Hungarian aristocrats, princes, countesses . . . A modern state cannot exist without informers. I shouldn't make such a fuss about it. I would only have to pass on some information about my co-workers from time to time, or about my acquaintances—who is friends with whom, who is lovers with whom, what are their political opinions, do they spend more than they make, do they write letters abroad . . . and so on and so forth."

She drank her cognac and looked at Marosi. Her eyes were almost clear. "I didn't want to do any of those things, but I couldn't get rid of those two. That's when I remembered Eva Szalánczky."

Marosi signaled the waitress. Magda Módra continued with her story. "I had read Eva's stories in the newspaper. She was one person who could not be compromised. I thought maybe she could help me. I went to see her, and I told her about my problems. She thought about it for a while, and then she said: 'Listen! First you call the minister of justice and ask him to listen to you. If he will see you, tell him everything exactly the same way you told me. Make it clear that you are not interested. You spent time in jail, and now you want to be left in peace. They'll find enough volunteers for their purposes. Enough! When the Germans occupied Budapest, the Gestapo received forty thousand denunciations during the first week. There is no need to worry that the people of Budapest will not be loyal towards whoever is in power . . . Yes, I know, 1956 was the exception . . . If the minister doesn't want to see you, for whatever reason, write him a letter. You can be sure that he'll make arrangements and that you'll be left alone . . . If not, come back to me and we'll think of something else.'"

They drank their cognacs.

"And that's what you did?" Marosi wanted to know.

"Yes," Magda Módra said. "I was no longer shadowed."

"And how did you get your job in the library?"

"I went to some of my former teachers and they took care of it."

"And Eva?"

Magda noisily drank the last drops from her glass. Marosi ordered again, but only for her. If he went on drinking, he would remember only that he was sitting with a drunk woman in a garden café, and nothing else.

"I fell in love with Eva . . . She was in bad shape then. We drank a lot together, and she allowed me to take her to her room, and she allowed me to take care of her . . . But she wasn't willing to engage in anything else."

"Why was she in bad shape?" Marosi asked.

"I don't know. She never talked about it. She was a very private human being. We mostly talked about literature. About Freud, Nietzsche's Zarathustra, about Sartre's existentialism . . . I loved her madly. Once, in desperation, I became very demanding and I asked her if she didn't love me because she thought I was an informer after all. 'I don't care if you are an informer, Magda,' she replied. 'What could you say about me? My most secret thoughts are in my stories. My greatest pain is that they are not printed, and no judge is questioning me about them. That would at least prove that I have thoughts. I would know, even though I am not an important person, that at least I could not be ignored. No, Magda, I simply do not love you. Please understand that!' 'Why do you spend time with me then?' I asked her. 'Because I am alone. My friends have been hung, or put into jail, and I haven't succeeded in making new connections. I have to talk to someone. Someone who doesn't waste her brains figuring out how much carrots cost on the market. That's the reason. But don't have any hopes!'"

Magda Módra's tongue was already heavy, she spoke haltingly, but she pulled herself together and smiled.

"Coffee?" Marosi asked.

"Thanks . . . Once she said that she would kill herself, but she could not bear the thought of bleeding, drowning, hanging or falling. 'Can't you get me some poison?' she asked me. 'I could,' I replied, 'but under one condition: that you make love to me once.' She said yes, and I organized some morphine.

"From where?" Marosi was shocked.

"That's not important . . . I gave it to her, and . . ."

They were both silent. The waitress brought the coffee.

"Drink it."

Magda took the coffee cup and brought it to her lips with trembling hands. A few drops got on her chin. Marosi gave her his handkerchief to wipe them off.

"Did she take it?" he asked.

"What?" She remembered. "The morphine? Yes."

"How do you know?"

Magda's speech was entangled. "Because I was concerned and went to check on her few days later. She cursed me terribly, and told me that I had cheated her . . . I hadn't given her a fatal dose . . . She had only slept for two days. She was disappointed with me and never wanted to see me again . . ."

Magda started to cry. Again Marosi gave her his handkerchief. She wiped her eyes and her nose. It was barely possible to understand her mumbling: "I really gave her morphine . . . but I didn't think that she would take it . . . I was happy that she was still alive . . . even though I had lost her." She was really crying now. Marosi thought: *I have no more handkerchiefs.* He paid and asked the waitress—who was not the least surprised about Magda Módra's condition—to call a cab. He put his arm around her and helped her into the cab.

"Can you give me your address?" he asked. Magda Módra mumbled her address and a second later she had fallen asleep. Tightly, Marosi put his arm around her, but he awakened her when they arrived in front of her house. He pulled her out of the cab, dragged her to the elevator and rang for the concierge. A man in a striped robe came shuffling along.

"She doesn't feel well," Marosi said and put ten forints in his hand. "What floor does she live on?"

"Third floor, first door," the man said with an expressionless face and took them up. Pointing at the door, he asked: "Shall I call a doctor?"

"I'm a doctor," Marosi replied, supporting Magda's weak body with one hand and searching her handbag with his other. He took out a set of keys and with one of them he opened the door to her flat. He pulled the woman in, turned on the light and, terrified, he stepped back. The flat was empty. A mattress with rumpled sheets was in the middle of the room, and on the walls, a few clothes hung from nails. In one corner of the flat, there was a disorganized pile of books. Marosi put the weak woman on the mattress, took off her shoes and her stockings, opened her bra and covered her with a sheet. He went through the flat. Kitchen, bath, hall—empty, there was not one chair in the flat.

"Who gave you this flat?" he woke her up. With closed eyes, she stretched her arms towards him.

"Come here," she whispered. "Come, take my hand. I love you, because you love Eva."

"Who gave you this flat? The ministry of the home department?" he pressed her.

"Does it matter?" Magda Módra moaned in pain. "Do

you think that I'm an informer?"

Marosi put a glass of water, an ash tray and some cigarettes on the floor right next to her, turned off the light, closed the door and threw in the key through a small, open window.

"My god," he said despondently, "my god, that's also our generation."

14

L ivia had been waiting for him. *Interesting,* Marosi thought, *that name fits her so little. She looks more like a Cleopatra, or a Medea or Lucretia.*

Her green silk nightgown emphasized the green of her eyes. A discreet rouge outlining the borders of her lips made them more lively, more voluptuous. For a second, Marosi had his heart in his mouth.

He kissed her hand and they smiled at each other. Then he sat down in the chair positioned for him at the head of the bed.

"How are you doing?" he asked warmly.

"I could be better, but I'm all right," Livia replied, pondering for a while. "I don't understand it, but I trust you. I talk as freely about my life with you as if I were talking to myself, or to a bottomless well, trusting that it will never echo. But, at the same time, I'm afraid to reveal my despair. My doctor says that I'm allowed to concentrate only on getting well. But how can I get well without understanding what happened to me? And why it happened? But is this at all interesting?"

She took her eyes off Marosi and looked straight ahead. Her hand moved restlessly up and down the faded comforter. "There is an old saying: 'Only someone with good reason commits a cardinal sin.'"

Marosi was disconcerted; he had also thought of these words.

"I think there is no worse sin," Livia continued, "than the one my husband committed against me . . . Even in

103

my dreams, I would not have thought that he would do such a thing. Even when he was threatening me . . . There has to be something terrible, something demonic about me for him to attack me. When I met him, he was an honest man. The writing in an obituary—'the best son, the most faithful husband, the kindest father'—sounds trivial, doesn't it? Well, until this attempted murder, that's how I would have described him. He had no objectionable passion . . .

"I've already told you about how I became his wife . . . Until I went to the province, four of us—my parents, my younger sister and I—shared a flat consisting of one room and a kitchen. There wasn't enough room for all of us. There was constant tension and fighting. It's impossible to lead a life of acquiescence. My husband got a flat. When we moved in, we had three mattresses and nails on the walls to hang up our clothes. A hammer, which we used to drive in the nails, and a corkscrew to open up bottles . . . As long as we shared fixing up the flat, our marriage wasn't bad . . . Whenever we got paid, we bought something . . . Do you know how pleasant it is to bring home a nice lamp, a mirror, a wall hanging? And fairly soon, there was a child . . . For some time, I didn't think that I was missing anything. Then . . ." She mulled over the memory, her forehead creased with wrinkles. "I liked working in the archive. At first, I was only a clerk. But I was also doing some interesting research. I met fascinating people. Then . . ." She glanced at Marosi. "For a long time a man had tried to get close to me.

"One evening, I accepted his invitation. After work, we sat in an espresso. He talked about his life. He had been in jail for four years during the Rákosi era. He had been arrested in the second wave of the Rajk trials, even though everyone knew by then that Rajk was innocent. He was the victim of a show trial—the same as Bucharin's trial in the Soviet Union. But the opposition in the Party had decided to stand up and defend themselves. The hearings were made public and testimony about the Party's illegal methods of control were broadcast on the radio. It's possible that there was a traitor among the opposition; it's possible that Rákosi didn't *know* of a conspiracy, only feared one—anyway, a closed trial was ordered, and all the testimony from the hearings was banned. Even the judge knew they were innocent. It was very exciting for me to listen to his stories. I was feverish.

"When I returned home, my husband was lolling on the couch dressed in a jogging suit, doing crossword puzzles. At that moment, I realized how fed up I was with this guy. Who knows how long I'd been feeling like this? Maybe I wouldn't have been bored if he hadn't been my husband, but just some fellow-traveler between Budapest and Nyiregyháza. He had a half-day supply of intellect and wit . . ."

Marosi used the short break to ask gently:

"You are such a beautiful woman—how come you couldn't find a suitable husband?"

Livia looked at him slowly, her eyes shining, a fine smile—coaxed by Marosi's compliment—beginning in the corners of her mouth.

"I did find him . . . Unfortunately, too late . . ." She turned her head away from Marosi. "He can't get divorced, because it's impossible to divorce a woman who stuck by you when you were in prison, and who had to give up her university career and work as a dishwasher in a restaurant . . . He owned a little weekend house behind János Hospital . . . My husband heard the gossip—in Budapest nothing remains a secret. One evening he demanded an accounting, and I denied everything. By this time, I was disgusted whenever he touched me or tried to approach me. I evaded him. He remained suspicious. One afternoon . . . my god, it was tasteless, disgusting . . . he followed us and was lying in wait. At the critical moment, he hammered on the door of the weekend house and . . ." She shook her head, unable to continue.

"When was that?" Marosi asked softly.

"When? . . . We were both working at the newspaper." She wasn't aware that she had said too much. ". . . It was a year ago."

"Did Eva Szalánczky work at the paper then?"

"Yes. She started right around that time . . . From then on, my husband and I quarreled constantly. He had changed so much; sometimes I could only look at him in disbelief. This was the husband and father who earned the platitudes in the obituary? Jealousy turned him into an inventive and persevering torturer. In the past, when we had fights—everyone has fights—he was the one who always came around and said: 'Not in front of the child.' Once the little one was asleep, our anger had fizzled out. But now he was no longer interested in the child. He yelled, mocked me, insulted me. If I lay down, he sat at the side of the couch and didn't let me sleep; he caressed me, choked me, flattered me, and was very rude with me. During that time, I was only able to rest at conferences, or in the car, or on my way somewhere in the province . . . I was so wound-up from being so tired—I felt like an over-wound screw. I promised him I'd break it off with the other man."

"Did you do it?"

"I couldn't do it right away . . . He couldn't do it either . . . Even though we had already been well on our way to a more adaptable, tension-free, but meaningful friendship . . . At that time, I was already interested in others . . . And then he caught us again." She looked at Marosi and asked for some lemonade. He supported her neck with his hand, and carefully gave her the drink. Physically, he felt that he couldn't remain indifferent towards this unhappy woman who had such a tragic fate.

Livia looked at the clock:

"I would like to talk about that one particular evening;

maybe there is enough time before the doctors make their rounds . . . We went home together. I stopped at my mother's to pick up the child. My sister and my aunt were there, too. Once again, there was something in the air, a heaviness—a mixture of a market hall, a church and a lady's club—I left quickly. I fed the child, gave her a bath, put her to bed and told her a story about a little good-for-nothing fellow. With her tiny hand, she clasped my finger and that's how she fell asleep.

"My husband sat in a chair listening to the radio and, with a malicious smile, he followed every move I made. His mean look irritated me, drove me mad, and I was afraid that these vulgar fights would start all over again.

I preferred to go into the kitchen. I took an article, which I had to turn in the next morning, with me. The first lines drew a blank, but then my heartbeat slowed and the pressure behind my temples eased. I started to concentrate. My husband followed me into the kitchen, sat down on a stool opposite me and looked at me. I closed my folder.

"'What do you want?' I asked him.

"'You.'

"'Leave me alone. I have work to do.'

"'You listen to me, sweetheart,' he said, tripping over his tongue. Only then did I realize he was drunk. 'As long as I live, you won't get away from me.'

"'You are drunk,' I said, 'go and sleep it off.'

"'I won't go.'

"'Then I'll go.'

"I went into the other room. He followed me, tore the manuscript out of my hands and yelled:

"'I know you! Do you think I'm an idiot? You only got married to me to escape that village. You love your comfort. This . . .' his sweeping arm pointed out the walls of the flat, 'you won't take with you. And I'll only leave if I'm carried out—feet first.'

"I got scared. Four years' work had been put into this

flat. And the objects in the flat needed one another. Clothes need to fill the closet; chairs need to circle the table; the counter needs dishes and the shelves, books. As much as objects are useless without each other, as much as we need them. There is the floor lamp made of wrought iron, the Gorka vase, the washing machine, a print by István Szönyi on the wall . . . these are not only everyday items or luxury goods, but ropes which tie us down. Or are they only threads? It's more difficult to disentangle a thousand threads than one single rope . . . Yes, but not quite so.

"'Well, then, I'll move out with the child,' I told him.

"'Not like that,' he said coldly. 'The child will stay with me.'

"'Cut out the threats.'

"'There is not one judge in all of Hungary who would give you child custody. You have committed adultery.'"

Marosi shook his head. *Incomprehensible*—he thought— *deceived husbands lack chivalry.*

"I got scared," Livia continued. "I hadn't thought about that. The child's mine. Without the child, my life wasn't worth anything.

"He believed that he had won. He came towards me, embraced me, forced me onto the couch. I was horrified by his touch, I tried in vain to escape him, he followed me.

"'Wait! Listen to me!' he said. 'Passion never lasts forever. Yours will fade out . . . I can wait. I love you so much, I can wait. Only allow me, to also . . .' He pressed my body into the couch, searched for my mouth. He had the smell of cheap liquor on his breath.

"'Leave me alone! I don't love you!'

"'But I love you!'

"'I'm disgusted with you.'

"'And I adore you when you kick me!'

"I collected all my strength and pushed him away. He fell on his knees, his face pale and distorted. Slowly, he got up; mechanically, he rubbed his pants legs as if he was trying to dust himself off.

"'I have other means,' he mumbled and took a gun out of his briefcase, looked down the muzzle, loudly opened the magazine, counted the bullets. 'Six,' he said and sat down. He put the gun on the table in front of him. His mouth was twisted with a spiteful grin. I laughed, but my voice sounded as if it was falling into an abyss. I was so terribly frightened.

"When he lit a cigarette, I pretended that I was going to the bathroom and left the room. I took my coat from the wardrobe, noiselessly opened the front door and closed it softly behind me.

"I was on the street in the middle of the night. What now? I thought of all my colleagues, all my acquaintances— I wasn't close enough to anyone to just knock on their door in the middle of the night . . . A terrible feeling . . ."

"And Eva Szalánczky?" Marosi asked cautiously.

"She was no longer in Budapest." She corrected herself: "She was and she wasn't. She had already quit the paper . . . On top of it, I didn't know her address . . . That left only my mother . . . Everybody in the one-room flat woke up. My mother held me responsible for everything. Her main argument was: 'Now that your sister is engaged, you want to get a divorce? Do you want to spoil her match? The two of them don't have a flat. Where can they live but here?' And so on. Market hall, church and lady's club."

Exhausted, Livia fell silent, but then she added with a bitter, grimace-like smile:

"I returned, hoping that he would calm down and not carry out his threat. Three months later he shot me."

The nurse appeared at the door—she was in a good mood and rambled along.

"May I come back tomorrow?" Marosi asked, when he kissed Livia's hand, holding it for a bit longer than usual.

"Do come."

15

Despite their appointment, Marosi did not find Major Blindics, the head of the homicide division, at the police station at the arranged time. He was probably on the road to do some site inspections in a new murder case. Life did not stand still, and neither did death. After reflecting briefly, Marosi went back home and decided to invite Cunika out for lunch. They could eat out either on Margaret Island or on Three Borders Hill. She was always upset at this time of the day, since she would have liked to spend it working at the film studios.

Cunika, still in her robe, was sitting on the floor, painting her toe nails. She was listening to soft dance music on the radio. She beamed when she heard his proposal, put her arms around his neck and said, pouting: "And I thought that you would come back after midnight, smelling of some other woman's cologne."

Marosi, who still felt Livia's hot hand on his lips—and who saw her tortured face, beautiful as a statue, and her long, smooth neck in front of him—didn't feel comfortable with Cunika's embrace. Softly, he pushed her away.

"Get dressed, dear."

Cunika curtsied.

"At your service, my First Lieutenant." She picked up her toiletries. "I haven't bathed yet. But it will only take eight minutes." Humming, she disappeared into the bathroom.

Marosi took off his jacket. He knew about Cunika's 'eight

minutes.' He took a stack of papers covered with writing out of Eva Szalánczky's landlady's bag. He put them on the dining room table, sat down and studied them carefully.

There was a ring at the door. Marosi pricked up his ears. Nine-thirty, maybe the mail. Should he open the door? From the bathroom there was splashing and happy humming.

Again, there was a ring, this time more impatient.

Marosi opened the bathroom door a bit.

"Cunika, there is someone at the door. Shall I open it?"

"No," said Cunika. She was in the water up to her neck. "Who knows who it is. If . . ." She faltered. "Give me my bathrobe."

She wrapped the bathrobe around her wet body, put on her slippers and left. Marosi returned to the room. He heard the turning of the key, a few words, and then Cunika appeared, pale in the doorway.

"Police," she said frightened. "They are looking for you."

"Me?" Marosi was surprised. "How do they know that I'm staying with you?"

"That's what you should know. Go!"

A square-built plainclothes policeman was waiting in the hall.

"First Lieutenant Marosi?"

"Yes."

"I'm police detective Lautner." He didn't offer Marosi his hand; he only showed him his card. Marosi looked at it, interested only in one item: Ministry of the Home Department.

"What do you want?" he asked sullenly.

The detective looked at Cunika:

"Would you mind, if we could talk in private . . .?"

A face that invites a beating, Marosi thought.

"Of course," Cunika said, offended and scared at the same time, and returned to the bathroom.

111

"What circumstances bring you to me?" Marosi inquired, and offered him a chair at the round table. Formally, they sat down.

"Did you ask permission to investigate the case of Eva Szalánczky?" Lautner asked in a harsh voice.

"Permission?" Marosi wondered. "What for? From whom?"

"Do your superiors know what you are doing?"

"Nothing concrete . . . But I asked for leave because of this case."

"What induced you to investigate on your own, parallel to police inquiries?"

"Inquiries?" Marosi smiled in agony. "I'm not inquiring, Comrade. I don't cross-examine anyone . . . I'm only talking with people."

The detective did not return the smile: "After you have scared them. Or do you think that everybody catches on right away that you are from the military, when you introduce yourself as 'first lieutenant'? No! Everybody thinks that you are from the police."

"I tell them right away that I'm from the border patrol, and that, unfortunately, someone who tried to cross the border illegally has been shot. Nobody can misinterpret that."

"Did you know if Eva Szalánczky had any connections abroad?"

"Well, excuse me!" Marosi was indignant, but he held himself back. Before he could say more, Lautner cut him off.

"Why did the concerned choose your district to cross the border illegally? Probably because she counted on your support?"

Marosi's stomach tightened.

"Since 1955, I haven't . . ."

"How long have you known Eva Szalánczky?"

"Since our school days."

"What did you do before 1956?"

Marosi remembered many of the old, degrading, bad-tasting interrogations regarding one's class background. But even then, no one dared talk to him in such a tone. He had been interrogated about an uncle who had frozen to death on the eastern front, fighting on the side of the Germans.

"Am I required to answer you?" he asked, suppressing his anger.

"If you don't answer here, then I'll have the right to summon you," the detective said with an expressionless face.

"Ask me," Marosi said, much at the other's mercy.

"What did you do before 1956?"

"I was supervising the mining of the western and southern borders."

"And 1956?"

"In March 1956, I asked for my discharge, after we had cleaned out all those mine fields which the floods had not swept into Austria. I hoped that my engineering services would never again be needed by the army. My request was granted, and I became a reservist. I tried to find work in the construction trades in my home county, but couldn't find a job matching my qualifications . . . At that time, nobody liked the secret police or the border patrol . . . I moved in with my mother and I designed one new cemetery and three bus waiting rooms for the city council . . . At the end of November 1956, I was drafted again. As you know, a number of active officers were compromised during the 'events,' and once again, the government needed people like me, who had not been involved."

"During that whole time period you were in contact with Eva Szalánczky?"

"No. We met for the last time in 1955, when we both finished our studies. I was sent to the province, and she remained in Budapest."

"As long as you were in contact with Eva Szalánczky, did

she ever ask you for your gun?"

Marosi was dismayed: "My gun? What for?"

"Suicide . . . It was her habit to ask her friends for a gun or poison."

All of a sudden everything became clear to Marosi. *The morphine. Magda Módra! An informer after all!* Early in the morning, once again sober, she probably had gotten scared and had run to her employer to report on their conversation as a way of preventing possible problems. Because of the morphine, the strange soldier could have caused her problems. She would have needed to report the source—this could only be a doctor or a pharmacy. A source which not only provided her this one dose, but which sold her drugs on a regular basis. He believed her capable of using all her money for drugs. That would explain why she hadn't even managed to buy a couch.

Marosi drew a deep breath. *What did Eva used to say? 'What can one report about me? I would like to reveal my deepest thoughts on radio so that millions can hear them.'* They could give him a good grilling, but they would not find anything compromising.

"No, she did not ask me for my gun," he said obligingly. "She also did not ask me to break my oath of office by helping her across the border. But if she had approached me with this request, I would have talked her out of defecting. Then she would not have been shot by one of my people."

"Why are you dealing with the case?" Lautner asked.

From this question, Marosi sensed a new insecurity in the detective. He became more relaxed, and propped up his elbows.

"Because I used to love this woman. I still love her. And that's why I want to know. What drives a young, twenty-nine-year-old woman from peasant background, with a university education, communist, considered talented, to see no other solution but to leave her country? It's because of this system! Even though it is no longer Rákosi's system, and no longer ruins the peasants or needs a state security police, it still instills fear! That's why!"

"Have you found any answers?"

"I already know one thing," Marosi said and prepared his counter-attack, ". . . it seems that the 'old' days are not yet over and they are still leaving traces."

The detective asked when Marosi would return to his unit, and how much longer he was planning on staying in Budapest.

"I'll stay another two or three days," Marosi answered and brought his discomforting visitor to the door. Without shaking hands, they parted.

He felt terrible. A miserable, frightened, blackmailed denouncer, a human wreck, was able to frustrate the absolutely legal and innocent plans of an army first lieutenant and engineer who was only motivated by his feelings! She could cause him trouble. *What an embarrassing half hour! To turn me into a suspect! What was that about? Is power based on such rabble?*

He walked up and down the hall, cursing softly. Then he took a bottle of cognac out of the bar.

"Unheard of! Goddamn nonsense! Such a parasitic worm is trusted? More than I? At least Metternich's informers were of a different caliber!"

Cunika came in. She was still wearing the wet bathrobe. Horrified, she stumbled and collapsed on a chair.

"How do they know that you are staying with me?" she asked in a hostile tone.

"I don't know," Marosi answered at a loss.

"To whom did you give my address?"

"Nobody . . . As far as I can remember."

"And my phone number?"

"Nobody . . . Do you want to have a cognac?"

She yelled hysterically:

"Who are they observing? You or me?"

Marosi put the cognac bottle and the glasses on the table, poured, and sat down across from Cunika.

"Drink . . . Did you listen?"

"Of course." Her lips trembled as she drank. "I heard that you are still in love with Eva. I'm pleased for her!"

"Cunika, right now this is not important. Calm down. I'm being observed." He thought about it. "Last night, I talked to a woman who is an informer. I remember that she went to the toilet once, and there is a phone there. I noticed it when I went there myself later. She could have called her employer from there, and since then they have obviously been following me."

"It's very comforting to know that," Cunika said, filled with rage.

"You heard that there was not a single word about you or about your husband," Marosi said, trying to calm her. Again, he filled the glasses to the rim.

"Not yet . . . But they are now opening files containing information that I'm receiving officers who are on duty at the border and who are suspected of smuggling people across. Everybody knows that my husband defected."

She screamed: "'And what is he doing abroad? How does he live? He betrays his country! And the wife of such a traitor . . .'"

"The divorced wife," Marosi tried to soothe her.

"Are you aware how many actors and artists were no longer given permission to work after 1956? How many were thrown into jail? How many were forced to flee jail and defect? . . . My husband left because they wanted to arrest him. Maybe he would have been hanged, like that unlucky filmmaker from the province!" Sobbing, she continued: "Do you remember Susanna Körösmezey? Did you ever see her on stage? She was a great tragic actress. When she played in Richard III, she thought Shakespeare was in the audience. That's how much she understood about politics.

"In October 1956, writers, actors, filmmakers assembled in Imre Nagy's hallway in parliament. All of a sudden, someone pulled in Susanna. The radio was broadcasting from there, because the prime minister was delivering a speech. After his speech, Susanna was given the microphone, and over the airwaves she said exactly what she had been told beforehand: 'I won't go back on stage as long as Russian troops are inside the country. Hungarian actors! Follow my example!' . . . They took her at her word: she hasn't been back on stage since." Cunika muffled her sobs. "My god! What an actress! I was still a student. When she performed in Richard III—I've seen her seven times as the Duchess of York—

'And being seated, and domestic broils
Clean over-blown, themselves, the conquerors,
Make war upon themselves; brother to brother,
Blood to blood, self against self: O, preposterous
And frantic outrage, end thy damned spleen;
Or let me die, to look on death no more!'

. . . everybody thought of the Rajk trial and there was thundering applause . . . And now . . ."

"And now?" Marosi filled the glasses.

"Delirium tremens."

In silence, they finished their cognac.

"All I need is to have my contract canceled," Cunika said and stared ahead of her.

"Don't be angry," Marosi said and felt ashamed. "I didn't want to compromise you. Shall I move out?"

She looked at him, her eyes red from crying:

"Typical, that you think of this solution, and not marriage."

Guilty, Marosi averted his eyes.

She sighed: "I know you still love Eva. Move to a hotel."

16

F ortunately, Marosi found a room in the third hotel he called. He put down his luggage, washed his hands and went to the dining room for lunch. His bad mood wasn't as bad as he would have supposed. He thought about Cunika's talented body with regret, but emotionally he felt nothing but comradeship for her. He was really sorry he had not met Livia Kismányoki six months earlier.

He went shopping at a nearby grocery store and then returned to his plain room. Once more, just to make sure, he called Major Blindics. He gave his name. If Blindics wanted to avoid him, at least he couldn't claim that he didn't know who called. The major said, as if justifying himself:

"I was told that you had been here. Unfortunately, our work forces us to be on call at all times; only in exceptional cases do murderers respect our schedules. Are you still going to be in Budapest tomorrow?"

"Yes."

"I'll be waiting for you in my office."

Marosi was relieved. Since he had no further plans for the day, he sat down, rolled up his sleeves, opened the cognac bottle and started to rummage about Eva Szalánczky's papers.

He discovered a few notes on Antal Szerb's *History of World Literature*. Within the text, he found only a few personal remarks: "When I passed my exams with honors, I went home and told myself: Now I will really start to study."

Then there were excerpts from Mihály Babits' *History of European Literature* and from Friedrich Nietzsche's *Thus Spoke Zarathustra*. One of the dialogues was underlined in red:

"When Zarathustra was thirty years old he left his home and the lake of his home and went into the mountains. He enjoyed his spirit and his solitude, and for ten years he did not tire of it . . . Zarathustra descended alone from the mountain . . . But when he came into the forest, all at once there stood before him an old man . . .

"'What do you want among the sleepers?'

"'I love man.'

"'. . . I love God; man is for me too imperfect a thing. Love of man would kill me.'"

Then there were Schopenhauer, Sartre, Weininger, Camus. Marosi had heard all these names; that's why he went on reading carefully, maybe he could learn something.

He had already switched on the light, when he came across an unsealed envelope without an address. He pulled out a few pages which were completely covered with typing.

"To the Press Control Office of the Ministry Council.

"Appeal.

"I, the undersigned, Eva Szalánczky, politely request the official in charge of the court of appeal to reconsider my work permit.

"I have the following reasons to support my request:

"In 1955, I graduated with straight A's in the history of literature from Lorand Eötvös University. I applied for and got a job at the weekly *Our Youth*. On January 1, 1957, the paper was ordered to close down, together with other newspapers, and has remained closed since then. The next day, new dailies and weeklies were organized. Of course, I wanted to continue working at a newspaper, and I immediately applied to the responsible authorities. Even though I wasn't known there—new people staffed the office and I hadn't been a journalist for very long—they took down my address and promised to contact me.

"Patiently, I waited for a few weeks; then I started to exercise some pressure. Especially, since my former colleagues and acquaintances, one after the other, got jobs at newly-founded publications.

"Finally, after three months, I was called for an interview. I was greeted by a comrade I didn't know. He asked me to sit down and then he opened a file.

"'Why didn't you finish your university studies?'

"This was his first question. You can imagine how shocked I was.

"'I finished! I graduated—with straight A's. If you want to, I can submit my diploma.'

"Yes?" he said, but he didn't seem surprised to find such a major error in my cadre file. Cold-bloodedly, he continued:

"'During the past years, you worked in Szeged, your home town, at the local newspaper. They were very disappointed with you there.'

"I felt uneasy. Whose cadre file was he looking at? With whom did he confuse me?

"'After graduation, I worked in Budapest with *Our Youth* magazine. I was not born in Szeged. I was born in a village near Szombathely. And I never worked with the local newspaper there," I said.

"The comrade didn't blink an eye.

"'You drink a lot and you behave scandalously in public,' he itemized.

"'This has also been reported from my "home town"?'

"'Yes,' he said indifferently.

"Now I was really nervous.

"'Why don't you understand? I've never worked in the province, and I only spend enough time in Szombathely to change from one train to the next.'

"I was talking to a wall. Who is responsible for entrusting such evil and stupid comrades with peoples' files?

"'You were kicked out of the Party in 1954, because of your immoral lifestyle,' he continued reading from the file.

"Right in front of me on the desk stood a massive glass ink pot. It was so old Jozsef Eötvös could have used it. It was filled with beautiful anthracite-colored ink. I was overcome by a barely restrained desire to throw that ink pot at him.

"'Comrade, why don't you understand? This is not my cadre file,' I said, trembling with pent-up anger. 'I wasn't kicked out of the Party. Currently I'm not a Party member, that's correct. But not because I was kicked out, but because the Hungarian Worker's Party, of which I was a member, has been dissolved and I didn't join the Hungarian Socialist Worker's Party. I wanted to keep my independence; in case the Party was wrong again, I would not be obliged to be wrong along with it . . . But I repeat: This is not my cadre file.'

"'What is your name?' he asked indifferently.

"'Eva Szalánczky.'

"'Eva Szalánczky. That's what's written here,' he said with unshakable composure.

"I felt that I either had to throw the ink pot at him, which would have meant the end of my journalism career, or that I had to run out. I opted for the latter. Since then, I regret not having thrown the ink pot at him . . .

"Who had messed up those files? In whose interest was it to put wrong information in those files? I'm talking about facts, not opinions. One can write that I believe or don't believe in god, that I'm disciplined or an anarchist, a communist or a revisionist—I could debate these characterizations. But graduation or not, that's not a question of opinion, that is a fact.

"The review board made a decision after more than one year, in April 1958. It was proven that I was not involved in any counter-revolutionary actions and therefore nothing was keeping me from being a member of the peoples' democratic press. The whole affair was over in ten minutes.

"But the whole thing had one flaw: there were six of us who had been called before the board and were waiting in the hall. I knew some of them; they were restless, didn't know why they had to wait—they should have been back at their desks in their editorial offices. 'You are working?' I asked, surprised. It turned out that all of them had work. 'Since when?' I asked. 'Right from the start.'

"How is this possible? The press law states that someone cannot be hired permanently as long as he or she has not been approved. Based on this law, I had been refused employment with several papers, among them the *Szombathely News* (I would have never worked there!). If this law isn't enforced, why are people referring to it? And if it's valid, why isn't it applied to everyone?

"An acquaintance—his hand is crippled, a hand grenade got him in 1945—took me aside.

"'Are you a Party member?'

"'No. I didn't join again.'

"'Well, we all re-joined.'

"In our country, all people are equal. But it seems there are some who are more equal . . ."

The writing ended there. It seemed as if Eva Szalánczky thought about it and didn't send off the appeal. Either she considered it a hopeless undertaking, or she was already working in Erdös' editorial office.

It had gotten dark outside. Marosi folded the appeal and put it in his wallet. He wanted to throw the notes on literature in the garbage can in his room. But he thought about it. They would be useful during the long hours of his night shift.

17

M ajor Dr. Blindics was a man in his forties who had put on too much weight. Behind his glasses, he had intelligent, lively eyes. He offered a chair to Marosi, who had come in uniform. Carefully, he listened all the way to the end of Marosi's story, which had become more polished, elaborate and convincing over the past few days.

He took off his glasses and wiped his eyes with a clean handkerchief.

"Yes, I understand . . . I've also dealt closely with the case of Eva Szalánczky . . . Especially after I heard about her death. Everything points in the direction of indirect suicide, even though the deed just doesn't seem to be in proportion to what preceded it. But what is proportion? A matchbox is small compared to the table, the table is small compared to Gellért Hill, and Gellért Hill is a dwarf in relation to the Himalayas. A standard measure for passion hasn't been found yet, and as long as we don't have one, who would dare judge whether this woman's feelings were out of proportion? And on top of it, humans not only exist in relation to each other, but also in relation to themselves . . ." He looked at Marosi. "Evidently, you knew Eva Szalánczky better than I did, since you were friends, and even close friends, in school. Correct me if I'm wrong . . . Here is a girl from peasant background; on top of it, Catholic, and so brought up with the strictest moral code. In other words, she is subjected to two complex systems of belief. This girl is in rebellion. She doesn't want to be a peasant, but an intellectual; not a Catholic, but a communist. One day, she discovers that she is a lesbian. That shakes her to the depths of her soul like an earthquake. Although . . . Isn't part of her rebellion wanting to a be a man rather than a woman? . . . According to today's scientific knowledge, these sexual practices have no provable biological, genetic or hormonal causes."

The phone on his desk rang. He picked it up: "Later," he said softly and put it down. "And as far as we know," he turned back to Marosi, "nobody is one hundred percent woman or man—or, someone so extremely one or the other would be considered pathological. Everybody switches back and forth between genders to varying degrees, depending on our partner at the time. The world Eva grew up in—not excepting school and university—considered every expression of sexuality 'outside the norm, a terrible sin,' and, frankly, they still do today. At the beginning, Eva wasn't willing to accept herself or resign herself to such attitudes. She went to doctors and psychologists for help. But since hers is not a disease, but a behavior, there is no cure. She had the choice of leading the life of an ascetic, passing up life's totality, or accepting herself." He looked at Marosi: ". . . Someone as capable of extreme passion as Eva, whose emotional scale ranges from utter devotion to suicide to the contemplation of murder, has no possibility of choice. We cannot go against our own grain. She couldn't do anything but give in. It was painful, she blamed herself and felt humiliated . . . Did she do it wholeheartedly? No. At some point she said to me: 'I'm a mistake of nature' . . . she thought of herself as stigmatized, marked."

He looked at Marosi and asked:

"Do I express myself clearly?"

"Yes," Marosi confirmed. "That's why she considered herself a tragic heroine."

"That's it." The Major took off his glasses, wiped his eyes

with his white handkerchief. Then he cleaned his glasses with a chamois cloth which he had taken out of his cigar box. He continued with more animation, inspired by the understanding he encountered.

"Inside, she was 'ready,' I would say, but then she had difficulties on the outside, the problem of finding a partner . . . What I'm saying now is based on empirical experience. I know of no—and I doubt it exists—scientific explanation. Besides their homosexuality, homosexuals have a lot of other problems in our society. Many are psychologically troubled; alcoholics and embezzlers, prostitutes, kept or blackmailed—I could go on. Without exaggerating, you could call it a subculture, where everybody knows everybody else, where partners are exchanged, and—this is very important—where everybody falls upon 'new meat,' consuming it at any cost, and transforming it into something that fits their own norms . . . I'm not talking about exceptions, such as great artists." The Major got up, stretched inconspicuously and went to the bar in the corner.

"Would you like some vodka?" When Marosi nodded, he continued. "It's not allowed during working hours, but I was the one who offered . . ." He smiled faintly, placed the already opened bottle and two glasses on the edge of the desk and poured. Marosi got up, they toasted and each returned to his side of the desk.

"I'll tell you about a few cases, so that you'll know a bit about this subculture. There is a forty-eight-year-old generally acclaimed engineer. He was homosexual in his youth. Then he got married, had two children. Normally, a middle-aged man exchanges his wife for a younger woman. But he fell in love with a seventeen-year-old boy. The boy was a typical Budapest prostitute who, together with a friend, lived off his earnings. They went to the friend's apartment, and the two of them charged the old fogy—that's how they referred to him—quite a bit for his secret pleasures. But one day, the engineer, thinking better, wanted to quit. The two of them didn't want to let go of him and started to blackmail him. For months, he allowed them to bully him, was afraid of the consequences in store for him from his work place and his family. The consequences wouldn't have been as severe as his fears. Ruined, he would have needed to sell his flat. That's when he killed the two boys."

Marosi whispered: "That's terrible." Involuntarily, he lowered his eyes.

The Major stopped when he saw Marosi's gesture. Again and again, he found that this wasn't as easily accepted for civilians—even if they were on military duty—as for those who deal with these cases on a daily basis. For a while he kept silent.

"Enough," he continued. "From even so little you can get an idea about the dark and sometimes dangerous side of this subculture . . . But what choice does a lesbian have?" His excitement changed his voice. "Unsatisfied women? Livia Horváths? Livia has a husband whom she doesn't love. She has a lover, but he is a bit too old. One night stands don't offer much of a future. Such a woman is like a carnivorous plant, she wants to eat every insect around her. Without consideration. The emphasis is on *without consideration* . . . She is not concerned with the consequences, or rather she can't even imagine them. It's difficult for people to imagine themselves in someone else's shoes, especially if their feet are too big; it's difficult to judge passion, especially a passion much bigger than one's own . . . Two starved women met in this editor's office. But Livia Horváth didn't know how much bigger Eva Szalánczky's hunger was than hers. Not only because of their different value systems, but also because Eva had to break through several layers of thick inhibitions and guilt. Eva made this desperate statement when I interrogated her: 'The bourgeoisie doesn't think that I'm toilet-trained.'"

"Comrade Major, are you angry with Livia?" Marosi asked.

Blindics stared at him.

"I'm angry with all the Hungarian intellectuals," he said full of rage. "These intellectuals do not live up to their standards. There have never been so many divorces, suicides, never so much alcoholism and so little work and success. Look closer at this case," his right arm shot straight out, the palm turned upward, as if carrying Livia Horváth's fate. "It's a reflection of countless cases, it's symptomatic, others just don't end as tragically. Everybody sleeps with everybody else, soon all of Budapest will turn into one big family. Whoever takes their own or anyone else's feelings seriously will pay a high price in this atmosphere of general promiscuity."

"Like Livia," Marosi said.

"No," the Major shook his head, "like Eva." He filled the two glasses. "Livia never took anything seriously. She is exclusively a victim of her own irresponsibility, her frivolity." He drank, and with a movement of his hand, he encouraged Marosi to do the same.

"She has recognized it now," Marosi excused her unintentionally.

"And paid far too high a price for it. Unfortunately not only her, but all three of them; only to realize something that most people know instinctively . . ." The Major was bitter. "Women who get you excited but don't put out are called teases where I am from. I come from Ferencváros, a suburban working class neighborhood, and there one takes revenge for such behavior . . ." He added quickly: "Not, that I would agree with that, but from a human point of view, I can understand it . . . Livia's husband did nothing but take revenge. But Eva Szalánczky's despair was directed against herself. At first she tried to commit suicide; when she failed, she left her secure job and went to the countryside. She fled."

"Was that when she decided to cross the border?" Marosi asked astonished.

"No. A few months later, the editor-in-chief called her back to the paper. She had been in Budapest for only two days when the tragedy happened."

Major Blindics took a thick folder out of his file cabinet, opened it, leafed through the pages, and then covered the folder with both palms. He looked at Marosi and continued his story:

"At two o'clock in the morning, Horváth called the police, saying that he shot his wife. I was on duty. When we arrived at the address he gave, the ambulance was already there, because Horváth had called them before calling us. Livia was conscious, but the doctor did not allow us to interrogate her. She needed immediate surgery. A shot through the lungs. They took her away. The man, the suspect, was dressed and sitting in his chair. He was calming down the three-year-old, who he held in his arms and who gradually stopped crying. He said with an apologetic smile: 'Let's wait for my mother-in-law. I called her and told her that a little accident had happened and that she should come over here to pick up the child.' We waited for her arrival, but didn't stay to listen to her screaming. We gave her the child and we took Horváth to the police station. I interrogated him. He stated what you already know, and gave us a letter, remarking that this was the last straw and caused him to attempt to kill his wife. The letter was from Eva Szalánczky; she had mailed it to his wife from the province. Livia wasn't at home, he received the letter and improperly opened it."

Major Blindics took a heavy, handwritten letter out of the folder and leafed through it. Marosi leaned over and saw lines of writing, marked up in red.

"That's the place." Blindics read aloud: "'This week I thought of killing you. But I don't dare get used to this idea, because once accustomed to it, I'll carry it out within two weeks. I'm not Horváth.'" The Major looked up. "Horváth maintains that this paragraph incited him to carry out his plan . . . Well, you know this goes a bit too far. Immediately, we went to Eva Szalánczky's flat. It was five-thirty in the morning. The landlady opened the door. She was in her robe, her hair was unkempt. We didn't find Eva in her room. The concierge said she had let her in around midnight, but she hadn't seen her leave. Where should we go and look for her? I thought that sooner or later she would hear what happened and would run to her girlfriend in the hospital. That's what happened. At eight in the morning, she ran right into our arms in the hospital's lobby."

Major Blindics continued to leaf through the folder.

"I interrogated her. She was nervous, hadn't slept enough, was hungover. She had a lit cigarette in her hand continuously.

"'Where were you early this morning?'

"'I had a nightmare and I woke up at around two. But getting up didn't help—the pressure inside me kept building and building . . .' Interesting," the Major injected, "the shot occurred exactly at two. 'I got dressed,' Eva continued her statement, 'and when the front door was opened for the day, I went out and strolled around the city.'

"'You already knew—'

"'No.'

"'When did you find out?'

"'Around eight, the editorial secretary called and she told me about it.'

"'What was your nightmare about?'

"'I was in some provincial town. Szeged or Mezötúr. Györ or Sávár. I don't know exactly where. What's important is that it was a provincial town, with a river cutting through it. Along the banks were woods, bushes, willows, and a path with yellow gravel. I walked along the path and by chance looked at the river. I stopped in dismay and stood rooted to the spot. There was no water in the river, but . . . How should I explain it? . . . Junk. Machines made out of iron, construction pieces; used, nude fragments, sculptures thrown in the garbage looking like skeletons. A frightening amount rose from the riverbed, in the place where the water usually overflows during floods. The mass of junk didn't stay in its bed, but moved on and on; as far as the eye could see there was only this rust, nude, almost transparent-looking iron mass. It was a construction reminding me of a horse skeleton made of leaders, harrows, burnt out tanks, iron wheels, and bent rails, but it was an indefinable, formless, iron monster. Numb, I stood at the edge of this wreckage-river and I knew: This is my life.'"

Marosi bit his lips, sighing heavily.

"Well," Major Blindics said, "a psychologist knows how to interpret this. I could only conclude that someone who has such a dream has destroyed everything she was born with, everything that had inhabited her life; but she was not able to create anything new . . . Then I continued the interrogation. 'Horváth shot his wife at two o'clock this morning,' I said. 'You left them at eleven, that's when the last bus runs. You were the last person who talked with both. Please tell me exactly what happened in your presence, what you heard and noticed. Everything is important in establishing the murderer's motives. Even more so, since we can't interrogate Livia Horváth.'

"'Is she going to live?' Eva Szalánczky asked.

"'According to the doctor who operated on her, she'll live' . . . I didn't give away that the bullet had also injured her spine, and that the outcome was uncertain. Eva seemed a bit relieved. 'So,' I went on, 'tell me about that last gathering.'

"'At ten in the morning, I went over to her house. We had arranged it by phone. Livia had told me that her husband would be on duty all morning. To my surprise Dönci opened the door.'

"'Horváth,' I corrected her. 'What did you want at Livia's?'

"'I had started to write something and I wanted Livia to read it.'"

"Where is this piece she started?" Marosi asked excitedly. Major Blindics shrugged his shoulders.

"I don't know. It wasn't in the Horváth flat. We searched there. Maybe it was in Eva's room."

That's possible, Marosi thought, *tonight I'll look through all her notes one more time.*

"'Dönci opened the door,' Eva went on, 'and when I asked for Livia, he pointed to the room, smiling his disgusting, sneaky grin. They have a one-room flat. You know it. I went in. Livia sat in the corner of the room on a chair and was crying. She held an electric cord firmly in her hand. 'That pig,' she said. 'That pig cut the cord from the reading lamp during the night. He wanted to strangle me with it. I was barely able to get it out of his hands . . .' I asked: 'Did you have another fight? Why don't you get a divorce and get out of this shit?'

"I interrupted her and asked: 'Did the two fight a lot?'

"'Constantly,' Eva said. "For months, Dönci has been threatening to shoot Livia. Fortunately, Livia is stronger, and she always manages to wrangle the gun out of his hand . . . Fortunately? . . . Did he shoot her while she was asleep?'

"'Yes. Please go on.'

"'When Dönci pointed so arrogantly at the door, he said: 'She can go wherever she wants to go. The flat and the child are mine.' I answered: 'Don't be so sure.' But he continued in his malicious way: 'Livia is the unfaithful one, the traitor, the adulteress. There is no reason why she should get the child if I insist on keeping her. The flat was given to me by the military.'

"Then," Major Blindics went on, "I asked Eva Szalánczky very calmly if she hated Horváth. Her eyes were flashing, she wanted to say something, but she lit a cigarette to buy some time. Then she went on:

"'Once, I told Livia to keep her husband's gun after one of these quarrels. She could take it to his superior and tell him honestly what was going on. But she didn't do it.'

"'Why do you think she didn't do it?'

"'There are probably several reasons. On the one hand, she didn't believe that he would carry out his threats—she considered them blackmail. On the other hand, she didn't want a scandal, didn't want her husband's expulsion from the military . . . He had a teaching credential, that's true, but not even a university professor earns as much as a teacher in the military . . . She was also afraid of her mother—*now, when your sister wants to get married, you turn your marriage into a scandal?*—After Dönci had made the remark about the flat and the child,' Eva went on, 'he put on his jacket, gave Livia a rough rap on the nose and left. In the doorway he said that he would be back at eight in the evening.'

"'The two of you were alone then?' I asked her.

"'No, we were three, the child was also there.'

"'How old is the child?'

"'Three years old.'

"'Continue.'

"Eva was thinking, looking at me questioningly.

"'Have you already interrogated Horváth?'

"'Of course.'

"'Did he tell you everything?'

"'If you are referring to Livia's lover, yes.'

'We talked about him too. Livia told me that she had gone to Margaret Island with him the previous day, Saturday afternoon. Dönci had shown up by chance and had made a scene in front of everybody. This was rather embarrassing, because the two had ended their affair three months before. Since the weather was nice, they decided to drink a beer out in the open air. But Dönci didn't believe that their affair was over, and . . . It was pretty delicate because Livia's friend is pretty well known.'

"'You can admit that it is Comrade Editor-in-chief,' I assured her. 'Horváth wasn't as discreet, he mentioned his name.'

"'Well then . . . Livia complained that Dönci had yelled that he would denounce the editor-in-chief to the Party's central committee and that Livia would have to quit her job at the paper.' Eva was silent. Her shoulders were hunched over, she had put both elbows on the table, her forehead buried in her hands. I waited for a second, then I asked:

"'Would you like to have some coffee?'

"'I'd prefer a beer, I have a stomach-ache.'

"'There's no alcohol at the cafeteria.'

"'For you, beer is already alcohol?' she asked with a tortured smile.

"'I can offer you vodka.'

"'No thanks, I don't want any alcohol now.'

"'Please go on.'

"'Livia was desperate. She didn't love Dönci, she downright despised him. But what could she do without a flat and without her child? She thought her problem unsolvable. I tried to calm her down, while I racked my brain to find a way out. I suggested that she go to the province for six months, possibly as a reporter for the *Pécs Newspaper*. I offered her my room, I would have gone home to my parents' village during that time period . . . Dönci wasn't really interested in the child. He used her to blackmail Livia. The child is being raised by the grandmother anyway . . . In short, we tried to find a solution . . . In the evening, at seven, Dönci returned home. We put the child to sleep, and I suggested that we go to the Béko, a restaurant. During the day it is an espresso, but in the evening it's a pub . . .'

"'Did you drink a lot?' I asked her.

"'I think quite a bit.'

"'How much?'

"'I don't know. But I think we emptied more glasses than could fit on the table.'

"'How big was the table?'

"'A little square table, the one commonly used in espressos.' She suggested the estimated size.

"'How much did you spend?'

"'I don't know. Dönci paid the bill.'

"'It would be important to know. You know that the influence of alcohol is an extenuating circumstance. Approximately, how much did he pay? Was it one hundred? Two hundred?'

"'I don't know. I probably wasn't at the table when he paid. I was busy with the jukebox all evening.'

"'Do you like music?'

"'Yes . . . And I found a record which I hadn't listened to since I was a teenager.'

"'What record was that?'

"'A rather stupid hit. A waltz. But . . .' she added almost excusingly, '. . . a certain part of my life is connected to it. Here's how it goes:

I waited for a word from you,
your lips remained sealed,
you didn't talk to me.
I looked into your eyes, you didn't dare
wish me kind words of farewell.
To leave me was nothing for you.
Pain stayed with me, it was very hard,
because I once loved you,
but it wasn't allowed, you heart breaker!'"

"I understand. When Horváth came home around seven, was he drunk?'

"'No. At least one would not have noticed it.'

"'And you and Livia?'

"'Well, we had drunk a bit.'

"'How much?'

"'I brought two deciliters of brandy, and she had as much at home. That's not much spread out over a day. And we did eat lunch.'

"'When did you leave the espresso?'

"Before eleven. I wanted to catch the last bus. Livia went home, she was worried about the child. Dönci took me to the bus stop. The bus had just arrived. I quickly got on it and went home.'

"'What did you talk about on the way to the bus stop?'

"'I don't think we talked.'

"'Think about it.'

"Eva was silent, then she said:

"'We didn't talk about anything essential. I would remember that.'

"'Horváth confessed. He told you at the bus stop that he would kill his wife that very night.'

"'Yes, he said something along those lines,' Eva admitted reluctantly. 'I didn't believe him. I thought that he was just babbling away. For months he had been threatening, why should he do it that night?'

"'What did you both say at the bus stop? Verbatim please.'

"'We stood there. All of a sudden, Dönci said: "I'll kill that carcass tonight." At that moment, the last bus arrived, I jumped on it and I yelled at him: "If you so much as touch a hair on her head, I'll be after you."'

"'What did you mean by that?'

"'I only said it, but I didn't think of anything specifically.'

"'You felt justified to make such threats?'

"'No.'

135

"'What was your relationship with Livia Horváth?'

"'I loved her, and . . . I would have liked to help her.'

"I looked closely at her while I continued with the interrogation: 'Horváth said that the child was downstairs in the yard playing with other children when he returned home at seven. The two of you were sitting in the dark room, kissing. Is that true?'

"'That's not true,' Eva replied vehemently. 'I was crying, and Livia was consoling me. He interpreted that wrong.'

"'You were crying? Not Livia?'

"'I've also got my own troubles.'

"'That I can believe,' I said and from my folder I pulled out the bulky envelope, the one I showed you earlier. She recognized it immediately and suddenly her face was completely bloodless.

"'You recognize this letter?' I asked her.

"'From what I can see, it's my handwriting,' she replied earnestly. 'How did you get it? Livia never received this letter. I thought it had gotten lost in the mail.'

"'You wrote to Livia Horváth: *This week I thought of killing you. But I don't dare get used to this idea, because once accustomed to it, I'll carry it out within two weeks. I'm not Horváth . . .* So tell me, what relationship did you have with this woman, if you threatened to kill her?'

"Immersed in her thoughts, she stared ahead and kept silent," Major Blindics continued. "I offered her some vodka, and she took it. She looked at me seriously for a long time:

"'Why should I lie to you? I'm in fact a mistake of nature. But not Livia.'

"'Did you two have a relationship?' I asked mercilessly.

"'No, no!' she protested passionately.

"'From what Horváth saw when he returned home, he had to conclude that his wife was involved with you . . .' She interrupted me:

"'He should have concluded the exact opposite. Who would sit in a chair kissing after pleasant lovemaking?'

"I didn't pay attention to her objection and continued where I had been interrupted: 'And that was going too far. That's why he shot her that night, and not three months earlier or two weeks later. Is that understood?'

"Then Eva broke down completely. She stared ahead with burnt-out eyes. I sent her out into the hall to wait until I had dictated the report. Mechanically, she obeyed. When I called her in to sign the statement, her hands were trembling so much she could barely write her name. On her way out, she turned around and asked:

"'Am I under arrest, Major?'

"'That's for the prosecutor to decide,' I replied.

"'If I'm charged, what paragraph will be applied to me?'

"'Conspiracy to commit murder.'"

Major Blindics was silent. He sighed and filled both glasses. They drank. Then Marosi asked:

"Is it possible that she wanted to escape prison?"

"I don't know," Blindics said helplessly. "Possibly prison, possibly her own guilty conscience . . . I'm still missing a link in the chain . . . possibly several links . . . We'll probably never know for sure." Seriously, he looked at Marosi. "What good does this knowledge do us, First Lieutenant? Where will it lead us? What do we achieve if we uncover one person's or one hundred peoples' secrets? Will it be easier to uncover the answers to our own lives? Isn't that sometimes harder? . . . Maybe you'll find out, or maybe you already know why Eva Szalánczky's life went downhill. What are you going to do with that knowledge?"

"I realize now how few things I understand about my own life," Marosi said thoughtfully. "Eva left in me, in my thoughts, a big hole, like a draft that makes you shiver and realize you feel like a failure at life . . . To every belief I had, she put a question mark . . . Possibly, I can free myself

137

of her now, can close a door that had been left open. But not in relation to the future, only in relation to the past. It doesn't pay to look back."

"Especially not at your age," Major Blindics said, stood up and extended his hand to Marosi. "Tell your soldiers never to open fire. Only if they have been fired upon should they fire back. Not everybody who is forced to leave their country is a saboteur, a spy, a deserter, a murderer out on warrant or a traitor of one's country."

"Understood," First Lieutenant Marosi said and saluted.

18

B ack on the street, Marosi remembered the letter he
had found in Eva Szalánczky's handbag—dated
Mohács, September 8th: "There is no explanation. One cuts
open one's veins . . . Someone else comes along who will
explain it."

It's possible, Marosi thought, *that this was a last message for
me. No, surely she didn't think of me . . . If she did, she might
have been tempted to contact me. She probably just needed someone
to explain it all. Is it an accident that this message reached me?
I don't think so. I'll try to give her an answer.*

19

First Lieutenant Marosi bought a paper and went to a nearby restaurant for lunch. When he saw the date, the food stuck in his throat. He had only one day left—tomorrow! The day after, he had to go back. He still had so much to do! He had to return Eva's landlady's bag. Then he had to figure out the rest of the phone numbers from her address book—maybe one of them would be the missing link in the chain. It would help to go to Eva's village, to see her brother—from there it would only be another fifteen kilometers to see *his* mother. He also wanted to hear the end of Livia's story—the severely injured needed an emotional accounting as much as physical healing . . . He panicked thinking that he didn't have enough time to finish all the tasks ahead of him.

He gulped down his meal and went to the hospital. Rest hour was over. Some patients, dressed in robes, walked up and down the halls, smoking; others gathered around beds, chatting.

Livia was lying motionless in her bed, the covers pulled up over her eyes.

Is she sleeping? Marosi wondered, standing right next to her. But then he heard a muffled sobbing under the covers. Carefully, he touched her shoulder.

"Livia . . . Please don't be angry . . . It's me. What's the matter?"

She wiped her eyes with the sheet, looked at Marosi, and hid her face again.

"I can't . . . Go . . . Please."

"What's the matter?" Concerned, he leaned over her.

"I'll never be well again," she said, the cover over her face. Jolting sobs interrupted her words. "There is no cure. My legs will remain lame . . . The bullet tore the motor nerves . . . My spine . . . maybe they'll sew it together and I'll at least be able to sit up. Do you understand? It's possible that I will be able sit . . . But destroyed nerves do not regenerate."

"But maybe they can be sewn together as well," Marosi said discouraged. "Today's neurological surgery is very advanced."

"Maybe . . ." she said, displeased. "The doctors also say that I have to be patient . . . But so far, there is no cure in sight."

Marosi felt a pain in his heart—the price was too high: one dead, one crippled, one convicted.

Livia's weeping was barely audible. Marosi put the first grapes of the season, the bottle of red wine and the newspaper on the night table.

"May I come back tomorrow morning?" he asked softly. "The day after tomorrow I'll have to leave. Unfortunately."

She was silent. She didn't remove the cover from her swollen eyes. Then she whispered:

"Come," and added: "Thank you."

Marosi thought he heard some regret in her voice. Most likely he had wanted to hear it.

20

M arosi went back to the hotel in a depressed mood. On the way, he bought a bottle of cognac, two bottles of wine and four bottles of beer. He didn't expect anything good to come of the rest of the day. This gloom, this sad state of consciousness reminded him of something ghostly. When he took off his jacket in his small, dirty hotel room, he remembered:

The summer of 1952. He had finished his service in Böhönye. To the ears of the Hungarian Peoples Army, "the Forest of Böhönye" sounded like the "Catastrophe of Mohács" or "Hiroshima." In the last days of World War II, a troop of German soldiers retreated into the forest outside Böhönye, surrounded themselves with a broad mine field, and waited for the Russians. But the Soviet troops did not want to bother with the destruction of a handful German soldiers. They surrounded the first mine field with a second one and moved on westward. When the Germans saw that they were hemmed in, they tried to get out of the forest. But they only knew the position of their own mines. They were all torn to pieces in the mine belt of the Soviet troops. In the early fifties, drafted Hungarian soldiers were ordered to clean the mine fields in Böhönye. They were assigned for one- or two-month tours of duty—nobody would have stayed longer. They had neither the German nor the Soviet mine plan. After 1945, the local people, who had gone into the forest for centuries to collect fire wood, were forced to go to a neighboring county for wood. Whoever went into the Böhönye forest after World War II did not return.

Marosi was platoon commander. He and his people lived

in the village. In the morning, they went out with their mine-sweepers, and when they returned in the evening, they had lost one or two men. The young soldiers' fear grew every day—Marosi's fear also increased—until it reached the stage of panic. Desertion, self-destruction, defection were the rule. Those caught trying to cross the border illegally in those days were accused not only of illegal border crossing, but also of spying and armed conspiracy. The sentence for that was death by hanging. Gábor Vaszary, the nephew of a well-known writer who was not allowed to study and instead had to work as an unskilled laborer, had escaped and had received a scholarship to the University of Maryland. With notice of this scholarship in his pocket, he had returned to Hungary and had tried to help two of his friends defect. They were caught and sentenced to death. Their fate was no different than the fate of the peasants' sons who tried to escape the mine fields of Böhönye.

Marosi found only a toothbrush glass in his hotel room. After trying to rinse out the taste of toothpaste, he poured himself a large cognac. He made himself comfortable right next to the phone. Again he had little luck. Businesses answered his calls; nobody knew the person he asked for. He reached a secondary school and the cleaning woman answered the phone; if he reached a residence, he was told that so-and-so wasn't living there and had never lived there. The sleepy receptionist at the Technical College dormitory asked:

"What room number?"

"Unfortunately, I don't know it."

"I don't know all four hundred students."

Most likely, Eva Szalánczky's acquaintance was no longer a student.

Finally, he got a husky woman's voice on the line. He imagined her soft body, her greasy skin.

"Good afternoon," he said. "I would like to talk to József Gyürki."

"József Gyürki?" the woman sounded surprised. "Who's calling?"

"I'm delivering a message from Eva Szalánczky," Marosi said.

There was a long silence. *Again nothing.* Marosi was angry. But then he heard the aggressive, mocking voice of the woman:

"From Eva Szalánczky? I can't believe it?!"

"Please, I . . ."

"You swindler!" the voice croaked. "You crook! Eva knows only too well that Jozsef won't be released for another fifteen years! Go to hell!" She slammed down the receiver.

Marosi wiped the sweat off his forehead and emptied the cognac glass.

Well, well.

Eva Szalánczky must have been very lonely after 1956. She had to start her life all over again. Marosi knew from his own experience how bitterly lonely it was and how much energy and time it took to form important and lasting friendships—and he had not considered himself an exile in Budapest.

Had only the events of the last few years motivated her to defect, or does the urge toward desertion, the sense of being an outsider, a stranger, homeless, date back further? Why had she cried ceaselessly into the freshly-ironed handkerchief of her classmate's mother? Was that the missing link in Major Blindics chain?

He took Eva's landlady's shopping bag and returned it to Verpeléti Street while he was still sober. But he was in no mood to meet the chatty, intrusive woman, and he left the bag along with a thank you note with the concierge. He walked back to the hotel, entering all the bars along the way. His depression did not go away. Back in the hotel room, he searched through what was left of Eva's notes. Four lines of poetry caught his attention:

As long as you are consumed by greed, you won't
have the rose.
Take the blackbird, happily singing in the foliage:
"I have spent myself with my song. I got drunk
on dew,
I'm full of cool figs. Couldn't you fall in love?"

Marosi sighed: "How true." He threw himself on the bed. *I have a terrible profession! A soldier must live and work as if his only task was to make himself redundant.*

He had been on duty in the border region once before, from 1951 to 1952. Since all Soviet-allied countries were boycotting Tito's political moves, the border with Yugoslavia had been legally sealed off. On their days off, the soldiers went to Farkasfa to frequent the bars and court the local girls. Marosi knew that village well. For decades it had a reputation as a rendezvous point for smuggling to neighboring Austria and Yugoslavia. One not only smuggled flints, medication, coffee, cocoa and gold, but also people. Especially people. It is possible that with the villagers' help, Western spies entered and left the country, but it was never proven, and not a single spy or courier was ever caught.

At the beginning of 1952, during a cold winter night, the secret state police from Budapest and Szombathely occupied the village—only security was left to the border patrol. Based on a list supposedly put together by the Party secretary Böske Szúró, an old limping bachelor, the secret police and their wolf dogs searched house after house and arrested seventy people. Among them, the former Party secretary, two local policemen, the midwife, the miller, a railroad employee, a farm laborer, and a kulak. Men and women. The entire family was removed from the last house. The son of another family—a soldier who spent his vacation at home—was also unrelentingly put on the truck. Under the protection of night, some men tried to escape across the Yugoslavian border. Marosi and his men shot them. The trucks brought seventy people to Szombathely. The following morning found blood tracks in the snow, a few corpses close to the border, and a village filled with desperate relatives and trembling neighbors. In the trials, ten people were sentenced to death.

Marosi drank the whole bottle. He wanted to kill all his emotions.

The border guards are still firing. There are still corpses in the forest, in the snow, in the furrows, in the mud. Has nothing changed?

After the events of 1956, the borders were left unguarded for six months. There were neither machine guns, nor electrical wires, nor wolf dogs. Two hundred thousand Hungarians chose the "free world." *Have we learned nothing from all the spilt blood? Do we still give people a reason to leave?*

Marosi thought that he would suffocate if he stayed alone with his thoughts. He got up, cleaned up a bit at the wash basin, and went out into the street.

Luckily, he encountered Fiala in the bar below the editor's office. The journalist was sitting at a corner table together with two other men. In the heavy smoke and under bad light, they talked discontentedly and with long silences. There were plenty of bottles on the table.

Marosi nodded toward Fiala, but sat down at another table. He ordered cognac.

Lazily, Fiala strolled over—he seemed a bit insecure—and patted Marosi on the back in greeting:

"Anything else of interest?"

"I don't want to disturb you," Marosi said, excusing himself, "but I would like to talk a bit."

"Oh, you don't disturb me," Fiala declined and sat down on the chair across from Marosi. "I see them every day. We take each other apart. Just talk. It won't be possible to take away my pleasure in living tonight . . . What are you drinking?" He ordered a bottle of red wine for himself. Marosi stuck to cognac.

"You know, my friend, I like women," Marosi said as a start.

"Well, at your age," Fiala said.

Marosi was happy because they both were at the same stage of drunkenness. They could remain on the same wave length.

"Are you from the countryside?" he asked.

"No," said Fiala, "I'm from Kolozsvár."

"Then you had a different experience. For a child from the village, sex is no secret. From very early on, you see pigeons, pigs, cows, dogs doing it . . . As Endre Ady says: 'At the age of five, I was no longer innocent . . .' Our favorite games were staging wedding ceremonies or playing Mommy-and-Daddy . . . I had just turned sixteen when the first grown-up woman, a war widow, pulled me into her bed. From then on, nothing which until then had been secret was kept from me. Do you remember the lack of men after the war?"

Fiala nodded.

"In the prisoner of war camp, where I was, there was a lack of women."

"Excuse me," Marosi said and changed the subject. "I met Eva Szalánczky when I was eighteen. The boys' and the girls' Gymnasiums gave a dance together. At that time, I had already had an affair with our physical education teacher. She spoiled me. I was a much desired little cock, that's for sure. I was bored at the dance, standing by a window and watching the dumb, immature teenagers. Then I saw a girl who was desired by all the boys. She wasn't very pretty, but she was an excellent dancer. Her movements had energy, ease and harmony all at the same time. 'What the hell,' I thought, 'she must be a ballet student.' I observed her for a long time, and then I asked her to dance. We mumbled our names. She really had a heavenly feeling for rhythm. I asked her: 'What do you want to do one day? Do you want to be a ballerina?'

"'No,' she said simply, 'I want to be Eva Szalánczky.'

"'What kind of profession is that,' I wondered. 'That's not a profession. That's me, or rather, that's what I'll be one day . . .' Now, my dear Fiala?"

With glassy eyes, Marosi looked at his past. He ordered another cognac. They drank.

"I was really attracted to her. After ten minutes, she told me that she had to catch the last train home. I was in boarding school and lived in the city. First I took her to the front door of the school, then to the street corner, and then to the railway station. I still couldn't separate from her, and I got on the unlit night train with her. There were only a few workers, sleeping, returning home from their shifts. I accompanied her to the village, almost to her home."

Fiala toasted him: "What did you talk about?"

Marosi drank and ordered another one.

"About farm work," he answered. "How much she disliked hoeing."

"That's it," Fiala nodded knowingly. "I would have also fallen in love with her right away."

"I wanted to kiss her in the dark train, but she didn't allow it. 'I don't even know who you are,' she said. There was no train back, and I walked the nine kilometers on the road. Day was breaking when I returned to the boarding school, and the opening May sky was as magical as the future."

Marosi poured some wine in a glass, continuing with his cognac as well.

"My friend, for the first time in my life, I was in love and I could hardly see her. Her mother was very strict and didn't allow her to stroll around the city after school. She had to take the first train back home. Then we had our last vacations before graduation. I didn't see her for weeks. The graduation banquet was again for both boys and girls. I didn't get anywhere there. I only found out that she was supposed to go to the youth recreation camp, and that she was going to work with the Hungarian Youth Movement. She had been appointed as the city secretary of this organization. After graduation, she wanted to study literature in Budapest." Marosi smiled. "I worked all summer and saved a bit of money and then went to Badacsony. From there, I swam across Lake Balaton to Fonyód. I had planned to arrive around eleven in the morning, so that the whole camp would be on the beach and could observe the little approaching point. I received much applause and envy when it was discovered that I was Eva Szalánczky's beau . . ." Marosi smiled bitterly.

"I didn't get anywhere . . . She was nice to me. After lunch, she brought a jelly sandwich to me on the beach. Nothing else . . ."

"Eva didn't like cakes," Fiala remarked.

"She also didn't like jelly sandwiches," Marosi said sadly.

"Maybe then she was still fond of them," Fiala tried to cheer him up.

"In the fall," Marosi continued, "we both went to Budapest to study. Two or three times a week I waited for her, either in front of the university or at the student cafeteria . . . Nothing . . . I seduced all her girlfriends, all her classmates, in the hope that she would find out about it. That's the reason why I seduced Cunika, because occasionally I saw them together."

"Who is Cunika?" asked Fiala.

"That's not important."

"Why didn't you tell Eva about your love?"

"I had done that in Fonyód."

"And?"

"She told me that I shouldn't bother."

"You didn't believe her?"

"No."

"Aren't you a bit too vain?" the journalist dug in a bit more.

"Possibly . . . But why should I have believed her?" He exchanged a glance with Fiala. "A few times, when I left Eva, I was in turmoil, dissatisfied. I went to one, two espressos, restaurants, just to look around. Each evening, I found a woman to take me home with her . . . Or to the so-called Hotel Mauthner: the underbrush . . . ."

". . . on Gellért Hill," Fiala interrupted him. "Hookers."

"Not hookers," Marosi corrected him. "Not all of them . . . I didn't have money for hookers . . . No, they were independent women. Widows, divorcees, girls from the textile factories. They didn't need money. Really. They cooked me dinner, mended the holes in my socks, sewed on my buttons."

Fiala was rolling with laughter. "In other words, you were a gigolo."

"No, that's not true," Marosi didn't permit it. "They were serious—I couldn't help it if they took me more seriously than I took them. I saw some of them again and again over the years." He poured some of Fiala's red wine in his glass, and sighed:

"There is no real replacement in life, my friend. You want one, you can have hundreds, but the hundreds cannot replace the one. That's really stupid!"

They drank again. Finally, Marosi's brain was fogged in. Maybe now he could talk about what he hadn't dared remember since then. Whenever it came to mind, he felt very ashamed.

"Once, I behaved really indecently . . . It was at a dance, a dance from the theater school. Cunika had invited us both. I had decided that I needed some resolution. I got drunk to get my courage up. I slept with a woman that afternoon, so that I wouldn't feel any desire later . . . at least not too much. As you know, Eva likes to dance. While dancing I told her: 'It's possible that the person I love in my imagination has as little to do with me as the stone lion guarding Chain Bridge. But I have no proof, and won't have any, as long as I haven't held you in my arms and haven't experienced what emotion may come: be it triumph, relief, liberation, happiness or nausea. It's possible that all the love I have devoted to you is nothing but a whim. But since I believe in this whim, my love is sincere. You are the symbol of my life, that's what you have turned into, and as long as you are not mine, nothing in life is mine. Why won't you do it with me?'

"'Because I don't love you, János,' she said seriously. 'If you want to know, I'm in love with someone else.'

"'Why don't you love me? Explain it to me!' I demanded from her.

"'There is no need for an explanation,' she smiled a bit. 'We are used to speaking like this: *The ancient Greeks knew: I am his friend because of who he is, and he is my friend because of who I am* . . . Well, in our case it's the opposite, and not even the ancient Greeks can make friendship possible between us. So much for that.'

"I became increasingly desperate," Marosi went on. By now the table was completely filled with glasses. "'I can't free myself, as long as you haven't given me an answer I can understand. A logical answer. That you don't love me is incomprehensible, illogical and unfair. What right do you have not to love me?' I asked her.

"'János, you are drunk,' she said angrily, 'take me back to my table.'

151

"'Couldn't you do it out of pity?' I begged her.

"Coldly, she looked me up and down:

"'You are not a soldier about to leave for the front,' she said and left me on the dance floor.

"I went to the bar and continued drinking. Then I got into a scuffle with a young guy with a mustache, because I had seen him dancing with Eva a few times. My dear Fiala," Marosi was roaring with laughter, "the ushers gave me a real good beating and then they kicked me out. I almost rolled down the stairs. 'Who invited that G.I.?' they yelled. I wasn't a G.I., but a student at the military academy."

They drank. Fiala said:

"Women don't like men who are vain and successful. Most of them think: *One woman this Don Juan didn't get is me.*"

"It was a good lesson for me. For years I didn't dare show my face to her. But I couldn't forget her. If I encountered something, let's say the smell of Virginia cigarettes in a railroad car's corridor—she had started to smoke Virginia cigarettes, but later switched to Munkás—or a blue-checkered tablecloth in a small-town tavern, or a bright white blouse, or really polished shoes, I bit my lips because of the pain, the shame and the helplessness. I had lost something without which the sky isn't high enough. My life became two-dimensional."

"You are really quite vain, my first lieutenant," Fiala said, drunk. "You are lacking nothing but humbleness."

Marosi was afraid he'd start to cry. He stuttered:

"Today I found out that I had offered her something, which didn't mean anything to her. There was something else in her life . . . But what good does this knowledge do me now? . . . I could be ten women . . . only to love her . . . But she's dead."

21

"**P**lease don't be angry with me about yesterday," Livia tried to smile at Marosi. "I was desperate." She had put some powder on her eyelids to cover up the red swelling from her tears. "I thought I would remain disabled, and I believed that my life no longer had meaning."

"What have the doctors said?" Marosi asked after sitting down on a chair next to her bed. He tried to cover up his hangover and his bad mood. Yesterday's pain was still there, he felt it, and there was a new pain when he thought that most probably this was his last conversation with this woman who had not deserved her fate.

"They will operate again. Three times if necessary. I'm not afraid of the pain, I'm only afraid that I'll remain disabled, dependent on others, a helpless burden." Her lips were quivering. "I'm still so young."

Softly, Marosi touched the back of her hand. *And Eva Szalánczky*, he thought, *wasn't she also young?*

"Yes, I know," said Livia, as if she had read this thought on his face, "I'm at least alive, but Eva . . ." She was silent for a while. "I want to believe that she didn't die because of me. Not for my sake."

"You told me once that Eva had tried to commit suicide," Marosi continued along the same line.

"I didn't think that she would really do it," Livia said thoughtfully. "I thought this would have been some kind of tug-of-war for her. That's what *she* was for me. That's

153

what I believed almost until the end. Pull and let go. When she pulled strongly, and I was in the orbit of her attraction, I'd scare myself and let go. Or better, I pushed her away from me. Under those circumstances, she came into my room and said: 'You only have to say one word and you are free. Are you going to say it?'

"'Yes,' I replied.

"'I have a dose of morphine. I'll go home and I'll take it.'

"'Do it,' I said and smiled at her in a friendly way.

"We didn't see each other for two days, but I wasn't worried. On the third day, she tumbled into the editor's office, pale, terrifying, looking like she had lost tons of weight.

"'It didn't work,' she said, subdued.

"'I don't believe that you did it,' I made fun of her.

"'I'm sorry that you can't attend my funeral tomorrow,' she said and left the room.

"I didn't see her for days. At the next weekly editorial meeting, the boss said that Eva hadn't renewed her contract and that she had quit the paper. Then I started to believe that she really had wanted to die. I felt a certain admiration for her. After the meeting, Erdös asked me in private if I knew why Eva had quit.

"'What did she tell you?' I asked him instead.

"'Nothing much. Only that she didn't feel comfortable here.'

"'And what is she going to do without a job?'

"'She told me that summer was approaching and she would go home to her village and try to do some serious writing. I tried to make it clear to her that this was foolish— she could write something serious here if she wanted to. She would only have to come to the office twice a week . . . But I couldn't convince her. She must have a serious reason to choose insecurity again after having been unemployed for a year and a half.' Erdös looked at me distrustfully, as if I knew more than I was saying."

Livia thought for a while.

"I had a guilty conscience. But there was already the second scandal with my husband, the threat with the gun, the electric cord, the knife. It hadn't helped that I . . . had broken off with the other man. My life turned into a complete hell. For some time, I forgot about Eva. She had left at the beginning of June, and in August I received a letter from her . . . It is in my handbag, on my night stand. Please take it out, dear Marosi."

Marosi took out the letter. It was the same shiny paper he had found in Eva's handbag . . . *Someone else comes along who will explain it.*

"Please, read the letter," Livia asked.

Marosi read:

"Livia!

"When I swallowed that morphine, I thought of Jesus, who was thirty years old when he revealed himself to humanity. I'll die at twenty-nine, because I don't want to reveal myself at the age of thirty.

"What followed you know.

"I went home, after deciding to extinguish the *you* inside me. I didn't succeed. For several reasons. One might be that your refusal wasn't clear enough. One can deny love in many different ways. Even in a decent way. The other reason . . . More about it later.

"A month ago, the film ripped. In my weakness and desperation, I wrote you a letter. The paper burned under my pen. If I had addressed it to the stone lion outside the opera, he would have filled with blood and come down from his pedestal in protest. But you remained firm and you didn't answer. I started to hate you. For two weeks, I waited for your answer. Then I got on the train, because I felt that this earth was too small for the two of us. If I couldn't succeed in killing myself, then at least I had to kill you.

"I called the editor's office from the railway station, but I was told that you were on vacation. I went to your flat, but you weren't there. I sat on a bench in the playground behind your house waiting for you to return so I could strangle you. It got dark. There were lights in all the other windows; only yours remained dark. I waited. For four days I sat on that bench, waiting. Apparently, I went home periodically, to take a bath, change my underwear, put on a clean blouse. I think I went to the espresso next to your house. I ate stale sandwiches and drank hard liquor. But for four days, I lived only to sit on a bench and wait for your return. On the fourth evening, once again, your windows remained dark, though there were lights in the other windows. I sat there like Simeon on the pillar and waited. At ten o'clock, the concierge turned out the light in the hallway and locked the front door. I sat on that bench. All of a sudden, I saw a light in the hallway and four men climbing up the stairs. Two guarded the first floor landing, while the others went up to the second floor, to your flat. They rang the bell, the door opened, and they disappeared into the flat. Police! The realization hit me: a murder had been committed. Breathless, I arrived at the house. I wanted to wait next to the front door to see if a body would be carried out. Who of the two of you had killed the other? But, in reality, there was no police car in front of the building. The front door was locked. There was no light in the hallway. There were no police. I came to my senses like coming up from under water and bobbing to the surface. I was frightened for myself. I went to the railway station and took the night train back to my village.

"Once you told me: 'Such a thing is sick.'

It's possible that it is sick,' I answered you. 'But that is secondary, and doesn't have more meaning than having TB or being near-sighted. What matters is if people are honest or dishonest. What kind of human being one is, is important, not whether one has tuberculosis or bad eyes. People don't commit sins in bed, but when they are fully dressed.'

"Once I had an acquaintance, a middle-aged woman. She committed suicide. She left the following farewell note on her table: 'I'm alone, that's why I became envious and hateful.'

"Livia, since my twentieth year, since I came to Budapest, I've been so alone, eagles could have built nests in my hair. I created a loose circle of friends at the university and at the paper. In 1956, this circle of friends fell apart. Some were hung, others were put in jail, and the rest left the country. The few who remained were like Lőrinc Szabó's characters: 'Those who heard the same story a week later, and believed that their complaints were new.'

"So far my life has been a never ending deprivation.

"I was deprived of work that would bring joy, and I was deprived of success, comfort, travel, a home and love. During the first twenty years of their lives, people should have twenty mothers, and in the following ten, twenty lovers . . .

"That's the second reason why something inside me clings to you, even though I know that love isn't the answer. I know love fades. The immense hunger inside me scared you and everyone else who, like you, lives on half-baked solutions. I hurt because of my emotions and you because of your pride.

"Don't think that I'm digging around my soul day and night. I don't have time for that. It's a pity that one doesn't need time to suffer, since suffering takes place in another dimension.

"My day here goes like this:

"My mother wakes me at six in the morning, after having milked the two cows. My father and my brother have been taking care of the animals since five. I put on shorts, sandals, my red striped shirt—the last time I saw someone wearing one like it was that coal dealer on King Louis

Street. I brush my teeth, wash my face, then I put the milk pitcher on my bicycle and bring it to the milk factory. On the way back, I do some shopping—if necessary. Then I make the beds. By that time, breakfast is ready. After eating, I either go with my brother to work in the fields—during the summer, the work includes hoeing, threshing, and so on; currently, we are busy with the fall chores, like gathering potatoes—or I stay at home to help my mother with the laundry (one of my aunts has a washing machine, but we don't have money for it), ironing, cleaning, and so on.

"Unfortunately, my mother always takes advantage of people. She made me clean out the chicken stable and whitewash it. I barely managed to get rid of the chicken lice. It's true she is thankful for help. She's aged quite a bit in these last years. When she is stitching, she even includes the printed price of 14,70 forint in the pattern. Often I feel her concerned, but also reproachful, glances: 'What's going to happen to you?' she seems to ask. Even though I didn't say anything about leaving the paper for good, and even though I kept my room, she feels instinctively that something is not right with me. Instead of staying in the village, and becoming a teacher or marrying the veterinarian, I chased after doubtful dreams in the sinful city.

"Before dinner, I wash myself with lukewarm water in the cement trough that has to be kept right next to the well in case of fire. After dinner, I have long talks with my brother in the kitchen. Rumor has it that in the fall producers' co-operatives will be implemented in our county. Everyone is talking about this problem. In the pub, in the milk factory, on Sundays in front of the church, and in our kitchen as well. Should my brother join or not? What else can he do? Work in a factory! I don't dare give him advice . . . He has to put his skin on the market, not I. On the winter night that ended so terribly, when you, Fiala and I went to Szolnok county to see the founding of a producers' co-operative, I despised that organization. How could factory workers, village mayors, teachers, librarians and the like dare persuade people of a different class to join a co-operative? Could they convince them? No! They tried to talk people into it, applying pressure by varying political and psychological means. They forced them to change a system which had taken root and developed over a hundred years, ever since serfdom had been abolished. What made them do this, since they knew only organizing, but nothing else, certainly not farm work? Is this courage or irresponsibility? I'm also convinced that a large enterprise is more profitable than a small one—but why does one not trust those who are directly concerned to change their destiny when they think the time is ripe for it? That's the least a democracy can offer.

"After our nightly talks, my brother goes to sleep, and I go to the room which I have all to myself, take out paper, pen and ink—and I'm overcome by despair. I'm like a far-away star, lonely and uninhabited.

"What will happen to me, Livia? Answer me!"

Marosi folded the letter and put it back in the envelope. He remained silent for a long time before asking:

"Why didn't the police confiscate this letter?"

"It was in my handbag when the ambulance took me away. They only asked me for my identification."

"You've kept that letter in your handbag since you received it?"

"Don't misinterpret it. I didn't want to tear it up, but I also didn't dare take it out of my bag, because Dönci was always spying on me."

"I understand."

"When I received the letter, I went to the editor-in-chief," Livia went on. "I told him that life in the country was ruining Eva, that she was in real danger of losing herself, and that, in the best case, she would end up as a teacher who is always at odds with herself. I asked him if it wouldn't be possible to invite her back to the paper. Erdös did feel a bit guilty, because he immediately agreed, gave me a car and sent me to Eva. I sent her a telegram because I didn't want to catch her by surprise . . ."

"You went there?"

"It would have been better if I hadn't gone," Livia reflected, "especially not alone, because Eva misunderstood the gesture . . . That was the week before all those terrible things happened. Eva came to Budapest on Saturday, she called me and we arranged for her to come to my house on Sunday. And then I woke up Sunday night, it was actually two o'clock Monday morning, when I felt a dull blow against my chest. When I touched it, my hand was all bloody."

"I know all those details," Marosi said.

"Please give me some lemonade," Livia asked.

Marosi gently put his hand behind her neck, lifted her beautiful head and put the glass to her lips. Even his hungover, weak body felt the impulses coming from this woman.

"Thanks," Livia said. Then she closed her eyes and continued: "You know, I would have been afraid of Eva, even if she had been a man." Marosi saw that she was really trying to express exactly what she felt.

"Eva was like a mine field," Livia went on, "crisscrossed with wires; wherever you touched them, they exploded . . .

"If someone was weaker than she—and I was weaker—then she would eat them, skin and bones and all . . . She liked to recite four lines from an Ady poem:

'We could accumulate much with our lies,
and Hungary would be flooded with success.
Credit to those who know how to keep silent!
But to confess everything, that was my reason
          for living.'

You know, she was in everything . . . somehow outside the law."

Yes, Marosi thought, *everyone is afraid for his own little life, scared of the invasion of destructive forces.*

"I would like to thank you," he said, "and please don't be angry with me for having disturbed you."

"I thank you." Livia opened her eyes, which seemed to be filled with tears. "You have given me an opportunity to take myself in my own hands like a complicated instrument whose workings I finally had to understand . . . Maybe it is not too late for me."

Marosi got up and took the woman's hot hand.

"May I write to you?" he asked. "I want to keep informed of your fate."

The smile in her eyes and on her lips was without courage, but hopeful at the same time.

"Write to me," she whispered thankfully.

Marosi leaned over to kiss her hand. But she pulled softly, yet determinedly, on his sun-tanned hand and offered him her lips.

22

"**O**ne tea with rum, please," Marosi said to the dining car waiter, then returned to looking out the window where the rain drops glided down quickly. The thin but steady rain made it difficult to distinguish the landscape from the heavy gray of the sky and the distant horizon. The express train to Mohács jolted through the impenetrable fall, depositing its smoke over the fields.

Marosi stared out at the discouraging landscape, the run-down corn and beet fields which reminded him of the border region. He was writing a letter in his head.

"Dear Magdolna Kóródi,

"Forgive me for sending this letter to you in Chicago, the city where you turned into a gun dealer. A male metier. As if you were a bike-racer. You know, cars don't have a gender, but bikes are male.

"I'm an old friend of Eva Szalánczky . . ."

The waiter placed a tea pot, a cup, and a half-deciliter of rum in front of him:

"At your service, First Lieutenant."

Marosi mixed the tea and rum. After a few gulps, he felt easier.

What can you do with your knowledge? he thought. Maybe it would be better to ask for a transfer to the Russian border, nobody there tries to cross illegally. Maybe it would be better to quit the service and go back to planning cemeteries. Maybe he should get married. When he tells his children about his life—about the war, then the first optimistic years after the war, and the long military service while he received his diploma, the events of 1956, Eva Szalánczky's senseless death—they might not listen half as much as when he tells them stories about the Turkish conquest of Hungary. Maybe . . . Maybe everything in his life will change.

He asked for another tea and rum and stared out the window, which by now was striped from the rain . . .

"I've been able to shed some light on Eva's life during the last year and a half," he continued the letter in his thoughts, "but it is not enough to understand her destiny. The two of you were classmates, you were friends for five years. Once, Eva cried in your mother's kitchen. Your mother was ironing and she gave Eva a fresh handkerchief. Why did Eva cry then? Would you know, by any chance? If you do, and if it wouldn't be too troublesome, would you mind writing to me about it?"

The waiter put the tea and the rum in front of him. For a second, he became aware of the soft sounds of the dining car, the clattering of the dishes. He mixed another tea and rum.

"Maybe she wanted to follow you to Chicago . . . Maybe she wanted to die. In Mohács, where she spent the night in a pub or on a bench in a waiting room, she wrote on a piece of paper: 'There is no explanation. One cuts open one's veins . . . Someone else comes along who will explain it . . .'

"Now I think she doubted whether an explanation was even possible. But I still hear a cry for help, and I think . . ."

He drank the rest of his tea and rum and looked out the window until he reached Mohács, as if waiting for the explanation behind the curtain of rain, beneath the thick haze, beyond the gray horizon.

GLOSSARY

Endre Ady (1877-1919): Hungarian poet. From a poor, Calvinist, but aristocratic family, Ady worked as a journalist in Debrecen and Nagyvarad rather than take over his father's estate. From 1904 to 1914, he was foreign correspondent for a Budapest daily in Paris. His poetry is considered to be among the earliest modern Hungarian poetry; Ady is regarded a forerunner of revolutionary socialist ideas.

Battle of Mohács: In 1526, the Ottoman Army defeated the Hungarian Army in Mohács, resulting in the occupation of large portions of Hungary by the Ottoman Empire until 1691. The battle of Mohács might have been won by the Hungarians if 50,000 peasants had not been slaughtered in the peasant revolt of 1514. Subsequently, Buda and Pest (Budapest, since 1872) were destroyed and the Sultan left the country with 150,000 prisoners, among them many women and children. This depopulation created the *puszta*, the empty, dried out wasteland between Tisza and Danube.

COMINFORM: Information Bureau of the Communist and Workers' Parties. Founded in Poland in September 1947, as a successor organization to the Communist International (COMINTERN) which was dissolved in 1943. The COMINFORM had member organizations from nine countries: the Soviet Union, Yugoslavia, Bulgaria, Poland, Romania, Hungary, Czechoslovakia, France and Italy. Since Yugoslavia's Tito was instrumental in founding the organization, Belgrade was selected as its headquarters. But after some disagreements, Tito and Yugoslavia were expelled and the headquarters were moved to Bucharest. The COMINFORM was discontinued in April 1956 during the process of de-Stalinization.

Hedwig Courths-Mahler (1867-1950): German writer who published more than 200 escapist romance novels, which sold extremely well and were translated into many languages. Some were made into films.

József Eötvös (1813-1871): Writer and politician. In 1848, he opposed the Hungarian revolution and supported the Habsburgs. In 1867, he was appointed minister of culture and education. Established compulsory education in Hungary.

Espresso: In contrast to more traditional and old-fashioned coffeehouses in Central Europe, which also served Turkish coffee, fast-food cafés opened in the fifties. They were called espressos, in reference to the newly-invented espresso machine.

Forint: Hungarian currency since August 1, 1946. In the fifties, 11.65 forint equaled one U.S. dollar; this exchange rate remained until the late seventies. In 1991, one U.S. dollar buys 80 forint. In 1956, a family of three required a minimum of 1400 forint to survive. But only 30 percent of Hungarian families had such an income: 55 percent earned less, and only 15 percent lived above this "poverty level." In a country with long, cold winters, 15 percent of the workers did not own a winter coat. While living standards had risen between 1945 and 1949, they declined nearly 20 percent in the early fifties, probably due to the country's industrialization efforts. Journalists were paid between 4,000 and 5,000 forint per month.

Julius Fučik (1903-1943): Czech writer and Communist Party member since 1920. His writings were well known throughout the Soviet-allied world. His *Reports Written Under the Gallows* has been published in more than 260 editions in 89 languages. He was hanged by the Nazis in 1943.

Attila József (1905-1937): One of Hungary's leading poets. His poetry deals with political and existential themes. Poor throughout his life. Joined the Communist Party in 1930 when it was still illegal. The party didn't approve of him and kicked him out. József, who was in and out of mental institutions throughout his life, threw himself in front of a train in 1937.

János Kádár (1912-1989): Leading Communist Party member and long-term Hungarian prime minister. Prior to his imprisonment (1951 to 1954), Kádár was minister of the interior under Rákosi. Became party secretary during the 1956 revolution, a position he held until 1988. In 1962, he said "He who is not against us, is for us."

Lajos Kossuth (1802-1894): Hungarian national revolutionary leader. His speech of March 3, 1848 started the Hungarian revolution. Austria suppressed that revolution with the help of the Russian Army. Kossuth went into exile in Turkey and later died in Italy. He is still considered the symbol of the modern Hungarian nation.

Kulak: Russian; farmer with more land than his family could till. Typically, kulaks hired employees to work the land. In the late twenties, Stalin persecuted kulaks in the Soviet Union by taking away their land and sending them to labor camps. The term *kulak* was used throughout Soviet-allied Europe as the process of forced collectivization spread after World War II.

Imre Nagy (1896-1958): Leading Communist Party member and Hungarian prime minister. During his Moscow emigration in the thirties and forties, Nagy was considered a liberal. In 1945, he was appointed minister of agriculture; in 1946, minister of the interior. Nagy was prime minister from 1953 to 1954. He was kicked out of the CP in 1955—

which split the party into two factions: followers of Rákosi and followers of Nagy. He was reappointed prime minister in 1956 during the uprising. Nagy was executed in June 1958.

Sándor Petőfi (1822-1849): Hungarian poet. His epic "János the Hero" (1845) relates the fantastic adventures of a peasant-soldier. "Rise, Magyar," written in 1848 voices the ideals of the Hungarian revolution in which Petőfi died.

Puszta in Winter: Information about this novel was unavailable; literal translation: Wasteland in Winter

Lászlo Rajk (1909-1949): One of Hungary's first Communist Party members. Unlike many other Party members, Rajk never lived in exile in Moscow. Fought in the Spanish Civil War. After 1945, minister of the interior, and then minister of foreign affairs. After Tito's exclusion from the COMINFORM in 1948, Rákosi wanted to prove his allegiance to Stalin. He accused Rajk, "the darling of the party," of conspiring with Tito and the West to re-establish capitalism in Hungary. He was also accused of having worked as an informer for Horthy and U.S. undercover agencies. During the show trial, Rajk, weakened by torture and psycho terror, admitted his guilt. The Rajk trial was the first in a series of large-scale imprisonments and show trials. On July 18, 1956, Rajk's corpse (or what was said to be his corpse) was put into a new grave and 250,000 people attended the ceremony. Right next to the grave stood those who had been put on trial with him but survived. Behind them stood the people from the central committee, who had ordered him hanged. This funeral was a major political event preceding the October uprising.

Mátyás Rákosi (1892-1971): One of Hungary's first Communist Party members. He was jailed in the twenties, but was released in exchange for Hungarian flags taken by the Russian Army during the 1848 Hungarian Revolution. Lived in the Soviet Union in the thirties and forties; returned after the Red Army had defeated the German Army in Hungary. Became secretary general of the Hungarian CP in 1945; was prime minister from 1949 to 1953, and from 1955 to July 1956, when he was forced to resign.

Stachanov (1906-1977): Russian miner. He set high, but totally unreasonable standards, which other workers were obliged to meet. Needless to say, the quality of many products suffered.

Lörinc Szabó (1900-1957): Hungarian poet and translator.

István Széchenyi (1791-1860): Founder of the Hungarian Academy. Instrumental in reviving the Hungarian language. At that time, the language of education was Latin, and the official language used for state affairs was German.

ABOUT THE AUTHOR

Erzsébet Galgóczi was born into a peasant family in a small village in Western Hungary in 1930. Teacher, factory worker, journalist, she began writing seriously in 1950, and won first prize in a writing contest that year. From 1950 to 1955, Galgóczi studied screenplay writing at the Academy of Dramatic Arts in Budapest. She then worked as a journalist and for a film studio in Budapest. From 1959 until her death in 1989, Galgóczi managed to write full time. She won the József Attila Award and the Kossuth Award for her writing.

Galgóczi started out as a committed Communist Party member, but over the years, she became more and more critical of the Party. She became one of Hungary's most important authors by writing about highly political issues while remaining true to her own vision. She was also politically active as a writer. She was named General Secretary of the Hungarian Writers' Union in 1979; she resigned in protest in 1987 when the Hungarian government refused promised tax reform for writers.

Another Love (*Törvényen belül*, 1980) expressed the belief that the uprising of 1956 was indeed a revolution, and not a counter-revolution as it was officially labeled. The novel also described the hardship of lesbian love in Hungary in the 1950s. The film version of the novel, *Another Way* (*Egymásra Nézve*, 1982), is viewed at lesbian and gay film festivals in the United States. *Another Love* is the best known of Galgóczi's many novels, screenplays and stories.

Erzsébet Galgóczi has been translated into several European languages; this is her first publication in English.

ABOUT THE TRANSLATORS

F elice Newman was born in New York in 1956. She is co-publisher of Cleis Press, which she helped start in 1980. She has worked in women's publishing since 1976, first with Motheroot Publications (Pittsburgh) and Out & Out Books (Brooklyn), and then with Cleis Press. Newman edited *Cameos: 12 Small Press Women Poets* (The Crossing Press, 1978) and co-edited *Fight Back! Feminist Resistance to Male Violence* (Cleis Press, 1981). In 1982, she co-edited the first issues of *Equal Time*, the Minneapolis/St. Paul gay/lesbian/bisexual newspaper. In addition to coordinating in-house editing, marketing, accounting and day-to-day operations of Cleis Press, she teaches writing at the University of Pittsburgh and, occasionally, journalism and communications at other colleges in the area.

I nes Rieder was born in Vienna in 1954. She has studied political science, anthropology, and social work, and works as a freelance writer and translator. Active in the international women's movement since the 1970s, she has worked with the Oakland-based People's Translation Service, publisher of *Newsfront International*. She was a member of the collective which produced *Second Class, Working Class*, an international feminist reader, and was a founder of *Connexions*, an international women's quarterly. Rieder co-edited *AIDS: The Women* (Cleis Press, 1988) and edited *Cosmopolis: Urban Stories by Women* (Cleis Press, 1990). She is currently writing a book about Central and Eastern European women after the fall of the Iron Curtain which will be published by Cleis Press.

Books from Cleis Press

Fiction

Another Love by Erzsébet Galgóczi. ISBN: 0-939416-52-2 24.95 cloth; ISBN: 0-939416-51-4 8.95 paper.

Cosmopolis: Urban Stories by Women edited by Ines Rieder. ISBN: 0-939416-36-0 24.95 cloth; ISBN: 0-939416-37-9 9.95 paper.

Night Train To Mother by Ronit Lentin. ISBN: 0-939416-29-8 24.95 cloth; ISBN: 0-939416-28-X 9.95 paper.

The One You Call Sister: New Women's Fiction edited by Paula Martinac. ISBN: 0-939416-30-1 24.95 cloth; ISBN: 0-939416031-X 9.95 paper.

Unholy Alliances: New Women's Fiction edited by Louise Rafkin. ISBN: 0-939416-14-X 21.95 cloth; ISBN: 0-939416-15-8 9.95 paper.

The Wall by Marlen Haushofer. ISBN: 0-939416-53-0 24.95 cloth; ISBN: 0-939416-54-9 9.95 paper.

Lesbian Studies

A Lesbian Love Advisor by Celeste West. ISBN: 0-939416-27-1 24.95 cloth; ISBN: 0-939416-26-3 9.95 paper.

Different Daughters: A Book by Mothers of Lesbians edited by Louise Rafkin. ISBN: 0-939416-12-3 21.95 cloth; ISBN: 0-939416-13-1 9.95 paper.

Different Mothers: Sons & Daughters of Lesbians Talk About Their Lives edited by Louise Rafkin. ISBN: 0-939416-40-9 24.95 cloth; ISBN: 0-939416-41-7 9.95 paper.

Long Way Home: The Odyssey of a Lesbian Mother and Her Children by Jeanne Jullion. ISBN: 0-939416-05-0 8.95 paper.

More Serious Pleasure: Lesbian Erotic Stories and Poetry edited by the Sheba Collective. ISBN: 0-939416-48-4 24.95 cloth; ISBN: 0-939416-47-6 9.95 paper.

Serious Pleasure: Lesbian Erotic Stories and Poetry edited by the Sheba Collective. ISBN: 0-939416-46-8 24.95 cloth; ISBN: 0-939416-45-X 9.95 paper.

Susie Sexpert's Lesbian Sex World by Susie Bright. ISBN: 0-939416-34-4 24.95 cloth; ISBN: 0-939416-35-2 9.95 paper.

Women's Studies

Peggy Deery: An Irish Family at War by Nell McCafferty. ISBN: 0-939416-38-7 24.95 cloth; ISBN: 0-939416-39-5 9.95 paper.

Sex Work: Writings by Women in the Sex Industry edited by Frédérique Delacoste and Priscilla Alexander. ISBN: 0-939416-10-7 24.95 cloth; ISBN: 0-939416-11-5 16.95 paper.

The Shape of Red: Insider/Outsider Reflections by Ruth Hubbard and Margaret Randall. ISBN: 0-939416-19-0 24.95 cloth; ISBN: 0-939416-18-2 9.95 paper.

Women & Honor: Some Notes on Lying by Adrienne Rich. ISBN: 0-939416-44-1 3.95 paper.

Health/Recovery Titles:

The Absence of the Dead Is Their Way of Appearing by Mary Winfrey Trautmann. ISBN: 0-939416-04-2 8.95 paper.

AIDS: The Women edited by Ines Rieder and Patricia Ruppelt. ISBN: 0-939416-20-4 24.95 cloth; ISBN: 0-939416-21-2 9.95 paper

Don't: A Woman's Word by Elly Danica. ISBN: 0-939416-23-9 21.95 cloth; ISBN: 0-939416-22-0 8.95 paper

1 in 3: Women with Cancer Confront an Epidemic edited by Judith Brady. ISBN: 0-939416-50-6 24.95 cloth; ISBN: 0-939416-49-2 10.95 paper.

Voices in the Night: Women Speaking About Incest edited by Toni A.H. McNaron and Yarrow Morgan. ISBN: 0-939416-02-6 9.95 paper.

With the Power of Each Breath: A Disabled Women's Anthology edited by Susan Browne, Debra Connors and Nanci Stern. ISBN: 0-939416-09-3 24.95 cloth; ISBN: 0-939416-06-9 10.95 paper.

Woman-Centered Pregnancy and Birth by the Federation of Feminist Women's Health Centers. ISBN: 0-939416-03-4 11.95 paper.

Animal Rights

And a Deer's Ear, Eagle's Song and Bear's Grace: Relationships Between Animals and Women edited by Theresa Corrigan and Stephanie T. Hoppe. ISBN: 0-939416-38-7 24.95 cloth; ISBN: 0-939416-39-5 9.95 paper.

With a Fly's Eye, Whale's Wit and Woman's Heart: Relationships Between Animals and Women edited by Theresa Corrigan and Stephanie T. Hoppe. ISBN: 0-939416-24-7 24.95 cloth; ISBN: 0-939416-25-5 9.95 paper.

Latin American Studies

Beyond the Border: A New Age in Latin American Women's Fiction edited by Nora Erro-Peralta and Caridad Silva-Núñez. ISBN: 0-939416-42-5 24.95 cloth; ISBN: 0-939416-43-3 12.95 paper.

The Little School: Tales of Disappearance and Survival in Argentina by Alicia Partnoy. ISBN: 0-939416-08-5 21.95 cloth; ISBN: 0-939416-07-7 9.95 paper.

You Can't Drown the Fire: Latin American Women Writing in Exile edited by Alicia Partnoy. ISBN: 0-939416-16-6 24.95 cloth; ISBN: 0-939416-17-4 9.95 paper.

Since 1980, Cleis Press has published progressive books by women. We welcome your order and will ship your books as quickly as possible. Individual orders must be prepaid (U.S. dollars only). Please add 15% shipping. PA residents add 6% sales tax. Mail orders: Cleis Press, PO Box 8933, Pittsburgh PA 15221. MasterCard and Visa orders: $25 minimum—include account number, exp. date, and signature. FAX your credit card order: (412) 937-1567. Or, phone us Mon-Fri, 9 am - 5 pm EST: (412) 937-1555.